青春绣像版中国古代四大名剧

The Famous Chinese Classical Plays

牡丹亭

Mudanting

原著：〔明〕汤显祖
改编： 李真瑜 邓凌源
翻译： 李子亮
绘画： 藤 茏

高等教育出版社·北京
HIGHER EDUCATION PRESS BEIJING

图书在版编目 (CIP) 数据

牡丹亭：汉英对照 / （明）汤显祖著；李真瑜，邓凌源改编；李子亮译 .—北京：高等教育出版社，2010. 7
（青春绣像版中国古代四大名剧）
ISBN 978-7-04-029664-8

Ⅰ . ①牡… Ⅱ . ①汤… ②李… ③邓… ④李… Ⅲ . ①传奇剧（戏曲）- 剧本 - 中国 - 明代 - 汉、英 Ⅳ . ① I237.2

中国版本图书馆 CIP 数据核字 (2010) 第 094124 号

策划编辑 吴学先
责任编辑 梅 咏
封面设计 于 涛
版式设计 于 涛
责任校对 刘 莉
责任印制 朱学忠

出版发行 高等教育出版社
社 址 北京市西城区德外大街 4 号
邮政编码 100120
购书热线 010-58581118
咨询电话 400-810-0598
网 址 http://www.hep.edu.cn http://www.hep.com.cn
经 销 蓝色畅想图书发行有限公司
网上订购 http://www.landraco.com http://www.landraco.com.cn
畅想教育 http://www.widedu.com
印 刷 北京信彩瑞禾印刷厂
开 本 880×1230 1/32
印 张 5.375
字 数 120 000
版 次 2010 年 7 月第 1 版
印 次 2010 年 7 月第 1 次印刷
定 价 19.80 元

物料号 29664-00

1.

【醉扶归】

你道翠生生出落的裙衫儿茜，艳晶晶花簪八宝填，可知我常一生儿爱好是天然。

恰三春好处无人见，不提防沉鱼落雁鸟惊喧，则怕的羞花闭月花愁颤……

Zuifugui (Drunkard Returning)

You observed my skirt shines with blushing red,
And hairpin sparkles with precious stones.
Do you know
My love of beauty is of natural build,
Like prudent spring charm lost to common eyes?
Once revealed,
Fish to the bottom dive,
Wild geese drop from the sky,
The moon conceals her face,
And flowers wink their bashful eyes
For with my beauty, they won't vie.

2.

【皂罗袍】

原来姹紫嫣红开遍，似这般都付与断井颓垣。良辰美景奈何天，赏心乐事谁家院。朝飞暮卷，云霞翠轩；雨丝风片，烟波画船……

Zaoluopao (A Black Robe)

Here the garden is all abloom in pink and red,
Yet all abandoned to dry wells and crumpling walls.
Enchanting sights on a fine day won't forever last.
Can any household claim undying joy?
Clouds that scud southward at the break of day
Bring back evening showers.
Rosy clouds, verdant cots.
Threads of rain, sheets of wind,
Misty waves and painted boats...

3.

【宜春令】

斜阳外，芳草涯，再无人有伶仃的爹妈。奴年二八，没包弹风藏叶里花。

为春归惹动嗟呀，瞥见你风神俊雅。无他，待和你剪烛临风，西窗闲话。

Yichunling (Spring Time Minitune)

West of the setting sun, at a remote place,

I reside with my aged parents.

I’m sixteen and a bud sheltered by patron leaves.

The ebbing spring had evoked in me a woe

And that’s why I caught sight of your face.

I come here for no other purpose

But to keep you company during the lengthy nights.

4.

【滴溜子】

神天的，神天的，盟香满爇。柳梦梅，柳梦梅，南安郡舍。遇了这佳人提挈作夫妻，生同室，死同穴。口不心齐，寿随香灭。

Diliuzi (Glassy Slippy)

Heaven above, the incense proves my words.

I am Liu Mengmei, sojourning in Nan’an.

This beauty by my side bestows me with her love

And we have decided to be husband and wife.

While we live, we shall live under one roof.

When we die, we shall lie in the same grave.

If I go against this vow,

I will expire with this burning incense stick.

前言

《牡丹亭》全名《牡丹亭还魂记》，是继《西厢记》之后又一部享誉天下的爱情剧，作者是明代著名戏剧家汤显祖。汤显祖（1550—1616），江西临川人。他一生正直，不肯依附权贵，四十九岁那年弃官回家，并在当年（1598）秋天写成《牡丹亭》。

《牡丹亭》描写青年女子杜丽娘受《诗经》中情歌的启发，萌动春心，在游园赏春后梦见书生柳梦梅，从此相思成疾，伤情而死。三年后，柳梦梅去临安赴试，经过丽娘墓地，丽娘幽魂出现，二人相会，丽娘在柳梦梅的帮助下，还魂再生，私自结合。丽娘复活后，父亲杜宝视女儿为妖孽，诬陷柳梦梅盗掘女儿坟墓。丽娘上朝申诉，柳梦梅金榜题名，皇帝做主，杜宝才承认了女儿的婚姻，全家团圆。

汤显祖认为：真诚的爱情是可以超越生死的。杜丽娘与柳梦梅的爱情，不再停留在反对父母之命、媒妁之言这一狭隘含义之内，而是具有战胜一切阻隔，超越生死的巨大力量。作者将追求自由爱情理解为“情”，将封建礼教理解为“理”，《牡丹亭》展现出“情”与“理”的冲突，以及“情”对“理”的最终胜利。

剧中的女主角杜丽娘是真情、至情的化身，她是一个热爱生活、追求自由、勇于反抗的青春少女，她性格中最大的特点是在追求爱情过程中表现出来的坚定执著。她为情而死，为情而生，无论是地府的阴森恐怖，父亲的专横冷漠，还是金銮殿的森严，都无法使她退缩，直至她取得最后的胜利。这就比《西厢记》中处处依靠红娘帮助的崔莺莺进了一大步。

剧中的其他人物也都个性鲜明。男主人公柳梦梅，既热衷功名又忠于爱情，他对杜丽娘的爱一往情深。杜宝的专横与固执，陈最良的迂腐，春香的调皮，也都刻画得非常深刻。

《牡丹亭》的艺术成就也是非常突出的。首先，该剧具有浓郁的浪漫主义特色。汤显祖将浪漫主义手法引入传奇创作，通过梦中相恋、死而复生、鬼魂成亲等一系列幻想情节，热情歌颂了青年男女对自由爱情与理想世界的强烈追求。其次，剧作在人物塑造方面注重展示人物的内心世界，发掘人物内心幽微细密的情感，通过刻画人物心理活动来塑造人物形象。杜丽娘的每次出场，每支曲辞，每个动作，都有着丰富的心理活动内容。第三，《牡丹亭》语言浓丽华艳，意境深远，充满灵动之气，洋溢着诗情画意，令人回味无穷。全剧采用抒情诗的笔法，倾泻人物的情感。如《惊梦》一出中【步步娇】、【皂罗袍】等曲子，直至今日，仍然脍炙人口。

据当时的文献记载，"《牡丹亭》一出，家传户诵，几令《西厢》减价"，并引起许多青年男女的共鸣。在舞台上，《牡丹亭》是盛演不衰的剧目，尤其是近年白先勇先生改编的昆曲"青春版"《牡丹亭》，使《牡丹亭》的艺术魅力在四百年后的舞台上大放异彩。

Introduction

The Peony Pavilion, or *The Return of the Soul at the Peony Pavilion* in full written by Tang Xianzu, a famous playwright of the Ming Dynasty, is another love story that enjoys worldwide popularity after *Romance of the Western Chamber*. Tang Xianzu (1550—1616) was a native of Linchuan, Jiangxi. As a man of integrity, he resolutely refused to become an appendage to the bigwigs and resigned from office and returned home at the age of forty-nine in 1598. In the fall of the same year he wrote *The Peony Pavilion*.

The Peony Pavilion describes a young girl by the name of Du Liniang who starts to have a longing for love at the arousal of the love song from *The Book of Songs*, and sees Liu Mengmei in her dream after visiting a garden in spring and since then becomes lovesick and dies of lovesickness. Three years later, while Liu Mengmei is passing by Du Liniang's tomb on his way to Lin'an to sit for the government examination, the soul of Du Liniang shows up and the two have a secret rendezvous. With the help of Liu Mengmei, Du Liniang revives from death and they get married without permission. After Du Liniang comes back to life, her father Du Bao sees his daughter as an evil spirit and accuses Liu Mengmei of robbing his daughter's tomb. Du Liniang goes to the imperial court to make an appeal. Liu Mengmei succeeds in the government examination. At the imperial decree, Du Bao gives approval to his daughter's marriage and the whole family gets reunited.

Tang Xianzu believes pure-hearted love can go beyond life and death. The love story of Du Liniang and Liu Mengmei is no longer limited to the narrow meaning of fighting against the dictates of parents and words of matchmakers. Instead the story shows love can be so powerful that it can conquer all and go beyond life and death. The author considers the pursuit of free love as "emotion" and the feudal code of ethics as "principle". *The Peony Pavilion* reveals the conflict between "emotion" and "principle" and the final victory of "emotion" over "principle".

Du Liniang, the heroine of the story, is the embodiment of true love and sincere emotion. She is a young girl who loves life, pursues freedom, and has the courage to revolt against conventions. The most significant trait that features her character is the firmness and obsession she evolves in the course of her seeking true love. She dies of love and gets reborn because of love. She never pulls back and continues to fight until she gets ultimate victory regardless of the eeriness and terror of the nether world, the peremptoriness and indifference of her father or the forbidding nature of the imperial court. This has been a great leap forward in comparison with Cui Yingying from *Romance of the Western Chamber* who has to count on Hongniang's assistance at many points.

The other characters in the play also have clear-cut personalities. The hero Liu Mengmei is both enthusiastic about pursuing an official position and faithful to love which is shown in that he is whole-heartedly devoted to Du Liniang. The peremptoriness and obstinacy of Du Bao, the pedantry of Chen Zuiliang, and the mischievousness of Chunxiang are also vividly portrayed.

The artistic merit of *The Peony Pavilion* is outstanding too. First, this play is permeated with a strong tint of romanticism. Tang Xianzu employs romantic techniques in his writing. By creating a series of intense fantastic plots like falling in love in a dream, returning to life after death, getting married to a ghost and etc., he warmly eulogizes the young couple's strong desire for pursuing free love and an ideal world. Secondly, in characterization, he attaches a lot more importance to revealing what's inside his characters' hearts and exploring the subtle and elaborate sentiments of the characters so as to create characters through describing their mental activities. Every single appearance on the stage of Du Liniang, every song and poem she chants and every action she makes all bear rich mental activities. Thirdly, the language of *The Peony Pavilion* is flowery and beautiful, brimming with poetic charms and a far-reaching artistic conception and leading the readers to endless aftertastes. The whole play adopts the technique of writing lyrics to depict the emotions of the figures as exemplified by the songs "Coy Steps", "A Black Robe" and etc. in the act "An Uninterrupted Dream", which are still very popular among people even today.

A historical document has it that "Soon after *The Peony Pavilion* is presented on the stage, it starts to be sung in every family and chanted in every house, almost overshadowing *Romance of the Western Chamber*," and striking an emotional accord with a great number of young men and women. *The Peony Pavilion* has remained popular on the stage for centuries. More than that, the "Youth Version" *kunqu* opera *The Peony Pavilion* adapted by Mr. Bai Xianyong in recent years in particular has made the artistic charm of *The Peony Pavilion* enjoy an even greater overwhelming popularity on the stage four hundred years later.

南宋（1127—1279）年间，西蜀有一位名儒叫杜宝，他是唐朝大诗人杜甫的后代。杜宝二十岁考中进士后，为官三十多年。三年前出任江西南安太守，为官清廉，美名远播。夫人甄氏，甄皇后家族的后裔。

夫妇二人相敬如宾，但年过五旬，膝下无子，只有一个独生女儿，名叫丽娘，芳年十六岁，长得端庄秀丽，聪明清俊，还没有许配人家。

杜宝视女儿如掌上明珠，一心想把她培养成贤德淑女。他专门给女儿请来一位老成持重的先生，每天教女儿读书，给女儿讲解《诗经》。

During the Southern Song Dynasty (1127—1279), there once lived a well-known scholar in southwestern China by the name of Du Bao, a descendant of the great Tang Dynasty poet Du Fu. Du Bao passed the advanced examinations and became a successful candidate in the highest imperial examinations at the age of twenty and had been in office for over thirty years. Three years ago, he was appointed as the magistrate of Nan'an Prefecture, Jiangxi. He governed Nan'an benevolently and incorruptibly and built up a good reputation among the people. His wife, nee Zhen, was a direct lineage of Empress Zhen of the Wei Dynasty.

The couple respected each other like guests, but regrettably they had no son. They only had one daughter named Liniang who was 16 years old. She was gifted and graceful and not yet engaged.

Du Bao treasured his daughter as a pearl on the palm and set his mind to educate her to be a fair lady of good and honest virtue. So he found an experienced and prudent scholar to teach his daughter to read books everyday and explain to her *The Book of Songs*.

这位教书先生名叫陈最良，是一个老秀才，饱读四书五经，但六十多岁了还没有考中举人，为人迂腐。

这天清晨，陈最良早早来到学堂，等了很久也不见杜小姐的身影，便起身叫道："春香，快请小姐出来听解书！"这才看到杜小姐素妆淡抹，带着小丫环春香，缓缓走进书堂。杜丽娘恭敬地向陈最良行礼，口里说道："先生万福！"陈最良一脸严肃地教导道："女孩子，应该鸡鸣起床，先向父母问安。如今你们正在读书，应当早起。"丽娘连忙答道："以后不敢了。"

The family tutor whom Du Bao engaged for his daughter was called Chen Zuiliang, an old *xiucai* who was well acquainted with *The Four Books* and *The Five Classics*. Though he was well over sixty, he had not passed the provincial examinations, and was rather pedantic.

Early one morning, Chen Zuiliang got to the family school. He waited and waited, but Du Liniang did not show up. He rose to his feet and shouted, "Chunxiang, ask your mistress to come for her lessons!" Soon Du Liniang, in fresh light make-up, strolled into the reading room followed by her maid Chunxiang. Du Liniang greeted Chen Zuiliang, saying, "Boundless happiness to my teacher!" Chen Zuiliang instructed her with a grave face, "To be a lady, you must get up when the cock first crows and ask after the health of your parents. At present your work is to study, and you must get up early." "I won't be late again," replied Du Liniang at once.

陈最良翻开《诗经》，问道："昨天讲的诗，你温习了吗？"丽娘答道："已经温习了。"陈最良开始讲解《关雎》这首诗，说："第一句'关关雎鸠'，雎鸠是一种鸟，关关呢，是鸟叫的声音……"小丫环春香才十三岁，非常顽皮，听到这里，便插话道："是怎样的叫声？"陈最良只好仰起头，学了一声鸟叫，乐得春香拍手大笑。

陈最良又讲解道："'窈窕淑女，君子好逑'，就是说那些幽娴女子，等待着君子好好地追求她。"① 春香听不懂，忍不住又问道："为什么好好地追求她？"陈最良无话回答，只好生气地说春香"多嘴"。

As he opened *The Book of Songs*, Chen Zuiliang asked, "Did you review the poem we learned yesterday?" "Yes, I did," answered Du Liniang. Chen Zuiliang started to explain the poem "Guan Guan Water Bird", saying, "The first line is 'Guan guan water bird, on the river isle.' Water bird is a bird, and guan guan is how it calls…" Chunxiang was only thirteen years old and was very mischievous. At this, she chipped in, "How does it call?" Chen Zuiliang had to look up and imitate bird call. Chunxiang clapped her hands and laughed aloud for joy.

Chen Zuiliang continued, "'Fair and slender girl, man asks for a wife.' That is, a quiet and gentle lady is waiting for a gentleman to come and beg for her favor nicely." Unable to understand what he was saying, Chunxiang couldn't help asking, "Why should he beg for her favor nicely?" Finding no fitting reply, Chen Zuiliang said angrily, "You're being too inquisitive!"

① "窈窕淑女，君子好逑"：这句诗的意思是，那些美丽的女子，是君子的好配偶。陈最良的解释是错误的。

丽娘插话道："先生，学生自己会依照注释读诗，您只需要把《诗经》大意讲解一番就行了。"陈最良听杜丽娘如此说，便长篇大论地讲了起来，道："这《诗经》三百篇里，有许多贤明后妃的故事，还有那催促丈夫早起的贤妻，远嫁他乡的淑女。用一句话概括，就是'无邪'两个字……"

陈最良滔滔不绝地叙说，春香早就不耐烦了，她借口上厕所，溜了出去。不久又一蹦一跳地回来了，她一进书堂便扯住丽娘的袖子，兴奋地说道："小姐啊，后面有个大花园，桃红柳绿的，好玩得很呢！"

Du Liniang said, "Teacher, I can read the notes myself. Could you give me an overall idea of the book?" Hearing this, Chen Zuiliang started speaking, "*The Book of Songs* consists of three hundred poems and contains many elegant teachings to exemplify a lady's life, such as the stories about the virtue of the queens and maids of honor, about the good wife who urged her husband to get up early and about a gentlewoman who was married far from her hometown. To sum them up, two words are just enough — 'no heresy' is what this book proclaims…"

Chuxiang had already been very much impatient with Chen Zuiliang's endless talking and had gone on the excuse of relieving herself. Soon she came back in a series of hops. Upon entering the reading room, she pulled at the edge of Du Liniang's sleeve and said excitedly, "I happened to have discovered a huge garden with lush trees and bright flowers. It's really a very nice place!"

陈最良一听就生气了，板着脸孔教训道："好啊，春香，你书也不读，居然跑到花园去玩！"拿起荆条要打春香。春香连忙藏到杜丽娘身后，分辩道："读书，读书，女孩子读那么多书干吗呀？"

陈最良心想，这丫头顽皮捣蛋，总是来引逗杜小姐，是该好好教训一下。他讲了一些古人刻苦攻读的例子，囊萤趁月，悬梁刺股等等。哪知话还没有说完，春香就反驳道："那有什么了不起的！悬了梁，会损害头发；刺了股，还会添伤疤呢！这不是自找罪受吗？"说罢，便又对丽娘说道："小姐你听，外面有人卖花呢！我们出去玩吧！"

This put Chen Zuiliang beside himself with anger. He scolded Chunxiang with a straight face, "Chunxiang, how dare you don't read your books and go and play in the garden!" So saying, he fetched a cane and was going to beat Chunxiang. Chunxiang hid herself behind Du Liniang at once and defended herself, "Reading, reading, what's the use of reading so many books for us girls?"

Chen Zuiliang thought to himself, "This girl is too naughty and often makes trouble to distract Du Liniang. Now it's time to teach her a lesson." He told Chunxiang that some accomplished scholars in the old days even read by the light of fireflies or by moonlight, one scholar even tied his hair to the beam and another one even stabbed his thigh in order to keep on reading. Before Chen Zuiliang could finish talking, Chunxiang refuted, "What's there to brag about! If one hangs his hair, he only hurts his hair! If one stabs himself, he only adds some scars! Isn't he asking for trouble?" Having said all this, she turned to Du Liniang and said, "My mistress, you hear the peddler hawking for flowers outside? Why don't we go out and have fun?"

这下可真的惹恼了陈最良，他再次举起手中的荆条要打春香。春香机灵地闪过身子，夺过陈最良手里的荆条，扔在地上，还顽皮地冲着陈最良做了一个鬼脸。丽娘看到事情闹大了，连忙责骂春香道：“死丫头，还不快向先生认错！”接着自己也向陈最良赔罪。

好不容易熬到了放学，丽娘等老师陈最良走后，便转过身来问道：“春香，你说的那座花园在哪里呢？有些什么景致啊？”春香兴奋地答道：“景致么，有亭台、秋千，还有太湖山石，名花异草，好玩得很呢！”丽娘低头沉吟了一下，没说什么，便带着春香回去了。

This really offended Chen Zuiliang. Once again Chen Zuiliang raised the cane in an attempt to beat Chunxiang. Chunxiang was quick-witted to dodge. Then she snatched the cane from Chen Zuiliang's hand and threw it onto the floor and made a funny face at him. Seeing that Chunxiang had messed things up, Du Liniang chided Chunxiang, saying, "You naughty girl! Come on quick and say sorry to Teacher!" So saying, she herself also made an apology to Chen Zuiliang.

Finally the class was over. After Chen Zuiliang left, Du Liniang asked Chunxiang, "Chunxiang, where is the garden you talked about? What views are there in the garden?" Chunxiang answered, "Views? There are pavilions, a couple of swings, a hill of Taihu rocks, priceless flowers and unnamable grasses. It's really a beautiful place!" Lowering her head, Du Liniang meditated in silence for a moment and went back to her room with Chunxiang.

从这天开始，杜丽娘和春香便每日早起，跟着陈最良读书。杜宝见女儿安心读书，心里非常高兴。当时正是春三月，远处传来布谷鸟的叫声，耕地播种的季节已经到了，杜宝想到自己身为太守，深居衙堂，不知道那些老百姓的农耕生产进行得怎样了，他决定下乡劝农。

杜丽娘和春香听到这个消息，乐不可支，尤其是春香。杜宝前脚刚走，她后脚就跑去告诉陈最良，说老爷下乡劝农，小姐也要请几天假，暂时不读书了。陈最良不敢多问，便回家去了。

From then on, Du Liniang and Chunxiang got up early everyday and read books under the guidance of Chen Zuiliang. Seeing that her daughter had set her mind on reading books, Du Bao felt very pleased. It was now mid-spring and the singing of cuckoos could be heard in the distance. It was time for cultivating the fields and sowing seeds. As the magistrate of Nan'an Prefecture, Du Bao had lived within the confinement of his office walls most of the time. He had no idea about how the villagers in his jurisdiction had been getting on with their farm work. He decided to tour his land.

Du Liniang and Chunxiang, especially Chunxiang were overjoyed at the news. Immediately after Du Bao left, Chunxiang ran to Chen Zuiliang and said, "My lord has been down in the country to inspect farm work for several days. And my mistress will take a few days off too. She won't be coming to class for the time being." Not daring to ask further questions, Chen Zuiliang left for home.

春香兴高采烈地回到闺房，她轻轻推开房门，卷起窗帘，只见小姐正在房中读书呢。丽娘看到春香进来，便放下书本，长叹一声道："'窈窕淑女，君子好逑'，圣人都这样说，真是今古同怀啊！"

春香见小姐面带倦色，便上前说道："小姐，老爷不在家，我们去后花园游玩一番，怎么样？"春香机灵地转动着眼珠，又说道："我已经跟老师请假了！"丽娘犹豫了好一会，才说道："大后天是个好日子，你去吩咐花郎，让他把后花园打扫一遍。"说罢又不放心地叮嘱道："春香，这事千万不要让夫人知道。"春香心领神会地点了点头。

Chunxiang returned in high spirits. She pushed open the door gently and rolled up the window curtains to find that Du Liniang was reading a book. Seeing Chunxiang coming into the room, Du Liniang put aside her book and, heaving a sigh, said, "'Fair and slender girl, man asks for a wife.' The sages' emotions are clearly revealed in these lines. Aren't these emotions shared by all people alike, be they ancient or present?"

Seeing Du Liniang look tired, Chunxiang went over to her and said, "My mistress, since your father has gone for a business trip, how about we go to the back garden and have fun there?" Rolling her eyes shrewdly, Chunxiang added, "I've asked Teacher for a leave and he has granted us permission!" After a moment of hesitation, Du Liniang said, "The day after next will be an auspicious day. Go and tell the gardener to sweep the trails and clear the garden." With that, she urged Chunxiang again and again, feeling a bit worried, "Chunxiang, never let my mother know about this matter." Chunxiang agreed with an understanding nod.

这天清晨，阵阵莺声燕语，将丽娘从睡梦中唤醒，她缓缓睁开蒙眬的双眼，伸了伸懒腰，披上衣服，掀开帷帐，只见昨夜点的沉香已经燃尽，微风拂动着湘帘，几缕晨光不知何时悄悄探入窗台，丽娘感叹道："剪不断，理还乱，闷无端！"

春香手里捧着盥洗用具，掀帘进来，说道："小姐快梳妆吧。"说罢取过菱花镜，伺候丽娘对镜梳妆。丽娘静坐窗前，凝视着镜中的自己，秀发如云，娇羞默默，真好比一枝迎风开放的杏花。连春香都在旁边赞叹道："小姐今天打扮得真漂亮！"

Early in the morning, the orioles aroused Du Liniang from her dream. Opening her drowsy eyes, Du Liniang stretched herself with a yawn, put on her clothes and lifted the draperies. The joss sticks had consumed themselves and the bamboo screen stirred in the gentle breeze. The light of the early morning sun had crept onto the windowsill. "Scissors have failed, combs are of no avail and all is tangled up!" Du Liniang sighed with emotion.

Holding toilet articles with both hands, Chunxiang entered through the bamboo screen and said, "My mistress, please get dressed up." Having said this, Chunxiang handed the mirror to Du Liniang and waited upon her while she dressed herself up in front of the mirror. Sitting by the window, Du Liniang looked at herself in the mirror. With beautiful hair falling about her and looking bashful, she is as charming as an apricot blossom joggling with the breeze. Even Chunxiang gasped in admiration, "My mistress, you look so beautiful today!"

丽娘矜持地笑了笑，她整了整头上的花，轻轻唱道：“你道翠生生出落的裙衫儿茜，艳晶晶花簪八宝填，可知我常一生儿爱好是天然。恰三春好处无人见，不提防沉鱼落雁鸟惊喧，则怕的

羞花闭月花愁颤……”①

主仆二人穿过曲槛，步履轻盈地来到花园门前。推开园门，丽娘迈了进去。园中绿树成荫，百花盛开，近处的假山，远处的亭台，都被阳光抹上了一层绚丽的色彩。

Du Liniang gave a restrained smile. Fixing the flower on her head, she chanted in a low voice:

"You observed my skirt shines with blushing red,
And hairpin sparkles with precious stones.
Do you know
My love of beauty is of natural build,
Like prudent spring charm lost to common eyes?
Once revealed,
Fish to the bottom dive,
Wild geese drop from the sky,
The moon conceals her face,
And flowers wink their bashful eyes
For with my beauty, they won't vie."

Passing through the winding balustrades, Du Liniang and Chunxiang came to the entrance of the garden in light steps. Pushing open the gate, Du Liniang entered the garden. It was covered with green trees and beautiful flowers. The rockwork nearby and the pavilions in the distance sparkled with a deep and mellow dye in the sunlight.

① 这支曲子的大意是：你说什么青翠的裙衫显得十分鲜艳，光彩绚烂的簪子用珍宝镶嵌，要知道爱美正是我一辈子的天性。却好像三春美景无人赏鉴，没想到我的美貌使得鱼沉雁落，鸟雀惊喧，使得花儿月儿都羞愧得颤抖。

丽娘从小在府中长大，还是第一次见到这么美丽的景色，她深深地陶醉在美妙的春光里，感叹道：“不到园林，怎知春色如

许！”她沿着花径一路前行，只见桃红柳绿，鸟语花香。水池中的金鱼轻快地摇着尾巴，树下一架秋千在微风中轻轻摆动，好像在感叹自己的寂寞。

丽娘心有所感，不禁对景抒怀，轻轻吟唱道：“原来姹紫嫣红开遍，似这般都付与断井颓垣。良辰美景奈何天，赏心乐事谁家院。朝飞暮卷，云霞翠轩；雨丝风片，烟波画船……”

As Du Liniang had been brought up in the confinement of her mansion, it was the first time for her to see such a beautiful view. Deeply enhanted in the spring scenery, she sighed with emotion, “If I didn’t come to the garden, how would I know spring could be like this!” Moving ahead along the path with flowers, she was carried away by the peach blossoms and green willow and songs of birds and scent of flowers. Goldfish were swimming freely in the pool, and a swing under a tree was swaying to and fro in the breeze, as though voicing its loneliness.

Deeply impressed by the scene, Du Liniang chanted:

“Here the garden is all abloom in pink and red,
Yet all abandoned to dry wells and crumpling walls.
Enchanting sights on a fine day won’t forever last.
Can any household claim undying joy?
Clouds that scud southward at the break of day
Bring back evening showers.
Rosy clouds, verdant cots.
Threads of rain, sheets of wind,
Misty waves and painted boats…”

春香站在花丛中，向丽娘招手道：“小姐你看，别的花儿都开了，只有牡丹还早呢。”丽娘向远处望去，只见满山的杜鹃花开得非常鲜艳，两只燕子由南至北轻盈地飞过。

丽娘深深吸了一口气，醉人的荼蘼花香立刻钻进了她的肺腑，让她心旌摇动，如痴如醉，她像是自言自语，又像是对这美丽的春光唱道：“遍青山啼红了杜鹃，荼蘼外烟丝醉软。牡丹虽好，他春归怎占的先？”

Standing amidst the flowers, Chunxiang waved to Du Liniang and said, “My mistress, come over and have a look. All the flowers are blooming except the peony. It’s now still a bit too early for the peony.” Du Liniang looked beyond into the distance and saw that the hills were covered with a burst of azalea flowers and two swallows were flying northward with ease.

Du Liniang took a deep breath and the fragrance of the flowers assailed her nostrils, making her feel intoxicated. Half to herself and half to the splendor of spring, she chanted, “Cuckoos have set the hills ablaze in a burst of azalea flowers. Beyond the roseleaf raspberry willow sprigs sway a tipsy dance. The peony is the queen of flowers, but how can it survive a retiring spring?”

面对此情此景，丽娘真是别有一番滋味在心头，这么美丽的景致，却被锁在这个大花园里，无人得见，真是让人遗憾。可自己的美好青春，不也是这样被埋没了吗？

回到闺房后，她的心情依然不能平静，自己已经不小了，却还是独守空闺，父母一心想在名门贵族中寻一段好姻缘，若嫁给那些纨绔子弟，岂不是白白地辜负了自己的花容月貌吗？这满腹心事和谁去诉说呢？

At this point, Du Liniang was filled with pathetic thoughts. She thought to herself, "The scenery is so beautiful, but is locked up in the garden and no one can enjoy it. What a terrible shame. Is not the beauty of my youth buried like this too?"

Coming back to her boudoir, she still found it hard to free herself from her disturbed mind. She thought to herself, "I'm no longer a child, but I'm still single. My parents just want to find a good marriage for me from among the distinguished families and noble houses. If they want me to marry a good-for-nothing young man from a wealthy family, wouldn't that be unworthy of my beauty? For whom can I pour out my cherished hopes?"

就这样胡思乱想着，她不知不觉地伏在书桌上睡着了。恍惚间，好像自己又来到了后花园，只见一个英俊潇洒的书生，手里拿着一枝柳条，向她款款走来。

那书生开口说道："小姐，原来你在这里，我到处找你呢。"丽娘连忙转过头去，含羞不语，心想，哪里来的书生，我和他素不相识，他来这里做什么呢？正在沉思之际，那书生又说道："听说小姐精通诗书，何不以柳枝为题，写一首诗？"说罢，便扯着丽娘的袖子，深情地说道："小姐花容月貌，真是让人怜惜啊！我真的非常爱你呢！"

As she went off into wild flights of fancy, she unknowingly dozed off, leaning on the table. In a trance, she seemed to have come to the back garden again. A handsome young man holding a willow branch came up to her leisurely.

The young man said, "So you're here, Miss. I've been searching for you high and low." Du Liniang looked aside at once and remained silent, feeling abashed, thinking to herself, "I've never met this man before. What's his purpose of coming here?" While Du Liniang was wondering who he was, this young man said, "I'm told you're well read. Why don't you compose a poem in the name of this branch?" Having said this, the young man pulled Du Liniang at the sleeve and said affectionately, "Miss, you're so beautiful! I'm madly in love with you!"

丽娘又惊又喜，欲言又止，那书生便牵了丽娘的手，向前走去。丽娘连忙停住脚步，含羞问道："秀才，你带我去哪里？"

那书生含笑不语，牵着丽娘的手转过芍药栏杆，来到湖山石边，牡丹亭畔。他将丽娘一把抱在怀里，说道："小姐，我对你爱慕已久了，你真是比天仙还要美丽啊！"丽娘非常害羞，想挣脱那书生的怀抱，那书生拥着丽娘，二人在牡丹亭畔卿卿我我。

过了一会儿，那书生无限深情地对丽娘说道："小姐，我走了，下次再来看你。"丽娘见书生要走，着急地呼唤道："秀才！秀才！"

With mixed feelings of surprise and joy, Du Liniang wished to speak but stopped on second thought. The young man took Du Liniang by the hand and moved forward. Du Liniang paused and asked with a shy look, "Where are you taking me to, Mr. Scholar?"

The young responded with smile but gave no reply. Taking Du Liniang by the hand, he led her to the Peony Pavilion by the Taihu rocks. He stepped forth and embraced Du Liniang, saying, "Miss, I've been in love with you for a long time. You're more beautiful than fairies!" Overwhelmed with bashfulness, Du Liniang tried to push him off, but to no avail. They let themselves go and made love at the Peony Pavilion.

After some time, the young man said to Du Liniang lovingly, "Miss, I'm leaving. I'll come back to see you." Seeing that the young man was leaving, Du Liniang called out, "Mr. Scholar, Mr. Scholar!"

耳边响起了母亲的声音："孩儿，你怎么在这里睡觉？"丽娘猛然惊醒，睁开眼睛一看，母亲正站在自己身边。原来是南柯一梦，丽娘顿时羞得满脸通红。老夫人数落了她几句，便转身走了。

丽娘送走母亲，只觉得出了一身冷汗，精神恍惚，郁郁寡欢。她闷闷不乐地躺在床上，一遍又一遍地回味着梦中的场景，那个手拿柳枝的书生，对自己何等怜爱！可是，现实中哪里去寻找这样一位知情知意的书生呢？想到这里，便觉得索然无味，这天晚上，丽娘翻来覆去，很晚都没睡着。

"My child, why are you sleeping here?" there came Mother's voice. Du Liniang woke up with a start and found her mother was standing beside her. Finding it nothing but an empty dream, Du Liniang blushed crimson. Mother poured a whole bag of words on her and then left.

After seeing her mother off, Du Liniang found herself soaked in cold sweat. Her mind started to waver, feeling very much depressed. Lying in bed in low spirits, she recollected the flavor of the happenings in her dream time and again. "That young scholar holding a willow branch in his hand," she thought, "how tender and affectionate he treated me! But where can I find such a young man who knows my heart so well?" With this, she felt pretty cheerless. That night Du Liniang tossed and turned and did not fall asleep until it was very late.

自从游园之后，丽娘就开始坐卧不宁茶饭不思了。她时时回忆起梦中的情景，不是长吁短叹，就是一个人默默地淌眼泪。春香也不知道是什么原因。

这天丽娘实在是忍不住了，便支开春香，瞒着老夫人，一个人偷偷地来到后花园，故地重游，再寻旧梦。一路行来，只见园门洞开，满地残红，不禁无限伤感。丽娘对景抒怀道："最撩人春色是今年，少甚么低就高来粉画垣，原来春心无处不飞悬。睡荼蘼抓住裙钗线，恰便是花似人心好处牵……"

The spring excursion brought Du Liniang onto pins and needles, making her have no appetite for food and drinks. Haunted by the happenings in her dream, she either sighed and groaned or wept alone. Chunxiang had not the least idea of why her mistress behaved so strangely.

Unable to take it any more, Du Liniang asked Chunxiang to leave her alone, and unbeknown to her mother, and slipped into the back garden for a search of her dream. Along the trail he came to the garden. Luckily the door was wide open. Seeing the fallen flowers on the ground, she was deeply moved and chanted:

"How tantalizing is this spring.
In spite of the enclosure of the painted walls,
Spring spills from the garden and floats about.
The sleepy raspberries are pulling at my skirt,
As if leading me to my lover's arms…"

湖山石边，牡丹亭畔，柳丝低垂，榆钱成串，雕栏外的芍药刚刚发芽，一切还是梦中的样子。丽娘不禁陷入遐想之中：还是那个眉目清俊的书生，还是那样含情脉脉的眼神，他轻轻牵着自己的手，来到这牡丹亭畔，他百般爱惜温存，气息是那样温暖，临走时的眼神是那样的恋恋不舍……丽娘不由自主地闭上双眼，口里喃喃念道："秀才，秀才……"

可是，当她睁开双眼，脑海中美丽的遐想完全消失了。眼前的牡丹亭、芍药栏，凄凉冷落，杳无人迹；那个手拿柳枝的梦中情人，不见踪影。

By the Taihu rocks stood the Peony Pavilion. There the willows trees were swaying in the spring breeze and the elm fruit was hanging there like strings of coins. The peony outside of the balustrades was in their first sprouts. All remained the same as it was like in her dream. Involuntarily Du Liniang got lost in wild and fanciful thoughts: Again that handsome young man, still as tender and affectionate as ever, takes her by the hand and leads her to the Peony Pavilion. He caresses her so tenderly in every possible way. His smell is so warm and so sweet. Look at the expression in his eyes, how unwilling he is to part with… Involuntarily Du Liniang closed her eyes and murmured with enchantment, "Scholar, Scholar…"

But all her daydreaming was gone when she opened her eyes. The Peony Pavilion and the balustrade porches were there, forlorn and desolate. All was quiet with no one around. No traces of her dream lover holding a willow branch could be found.

丽娘觉得自己是那样寂寞，天地这么宽，何处去寻找这个多情的书生呢？自己的一腔心事，究竟该托付给谁呢？她漫无目的地在园中徘徊，心里充满了孤寞与绝望。

不远处有一棵大梅树，杜丽娘走过去，梅树翠盖如伞，清香袭人，颗颗梅子挂满枝头，累累可爱。丽娘心想，自己死后若能葬在这梅树之下，也算是一个理想的归宿了。

Du Liniang was haunted by loneliness. The world was so vast. Where was she going to locate this amorous young man, and to whom was she going to commit herself? She hung around in the garden aimlessly, her heart filled with solitude and depression.

Suddenly she noticed a giant plum tree loaded with lovely and fragrant plums. Its sunshade crown stretched out wide and proud. "How lovely this plum tree is!" she thought. "I'll be happy to be buried beneath it after I die."

寻梦不成，丽娘的情绪更加低落了，整日愁眉不展，寝食不安。春香看在眼里，急在心里，劝说道："小姐，你以后再也不要去花园了，你自从游了花园之后，就精神不好，都瘦得不成人样了。"

丽娘听说，取过镜子，果然，镜中的自己好比一朵秋霜打过的残菊，消瘦了一大圈。她大吃一惊，眼泪簌簌落下，心想：秀才啊，我竟然为你消瘦到了这个样子！我若不趁此时把自己的容颜描画出来，等死了之后，还有谁知道我的如花美貌呢！她吩咐春香取来素绢、丹青，照着镜子，一笔一画地描摹起自己的容颜来。

With the pursuit of her dream proving fruitless, Du Liniang became even more depressed and lost both appetite and sleep. Chunxiang saw this and felt very much worried, saying to her, "My mistress, I suggest you make no more visits to the garden. Your two visits to the garden have worn you out a lot and you're losing weight."

At this, Du Liniang looked into the mirror and, to her surprise, found that he had got so thinner, like a withered chrysanthemum beaten by frost. Tears rolled her cheeks. She thought, "Scholar, I've suffered such a significant weight loss because of missing you! If I don't catch this last chance and draw a portrait of myself, who will believe there has ever been such a beauty once death arrives?" So thinking, she told Chunxiang to fetch her a piece of snow-white silk, brushes and the colors. Looking in the mirror, she started to draw a portrait of herself one stroke after another.

镜中的自己，虽然消瘦了很多，但樱桃小口，柳叶细眉，秀发如云，眼送秋波，还是依然秀美。她细细描画着，想为自己画一个最美丽、最真实的形象。良久，画像完成了，只见画中人手捻青梅，面带微笑，亭亭玉立在湖山石畔。

春香一看，连忙拍手赞道："小姐画得真是像极了！只可惜少个姐夫站在旁边！"这话又勾起了丽娘的愁肠，她想道：梦中的书生手折柳枝，要我题诗，莫非我将来嫁的人姓柳？她提起笔来，在画像旁题了一首诗："近睹分明似俨然，远观自在若飞仙。他年得傍蟾宫客，不在梅边在柳边。"①

It was true that she had grown thinner, but she was still as beautiful and charming as ever with her cherry-like mouth, willow leaf-shaped eyebrows, fluffy hair and a pair of beautiful eyes. She painted meticulously, trying to produce the most beautiful and truest image of herself. After some time the portrait was done: a girl with a green plum in her hand and wearing a smile on her face stands gracefully by the Taihu rocks.

Seeing the portrait, Chunxiang clapped her hands and applauded, "It's a perfect reflection of yourself! Unfortunately, there is not a handsome groom by her side!" Chunxiang's words again aroused Du Liniang's sadness. Du Liniang thought to herself, "The young scholar in my dream held a willow branch in his hand and asked me to write a poem. Could that be a prophecy that my future husband will be a Mr. Liu?" So thinking, she picked up a brush and wrote a poem with a hidden meaning in the top corner:

"A closer inspection will proclaim her real,
But from afar she looks like an airy sylph.
If she is to meet with a scholar,
It must be by a willow instead of a plum."

---

① 这首诗的大意是：近看画像和人非常相似，远看则像一个自由自在的仙女。我以后若是嫁一个读书人，不是姓梅的而是姓柳的。

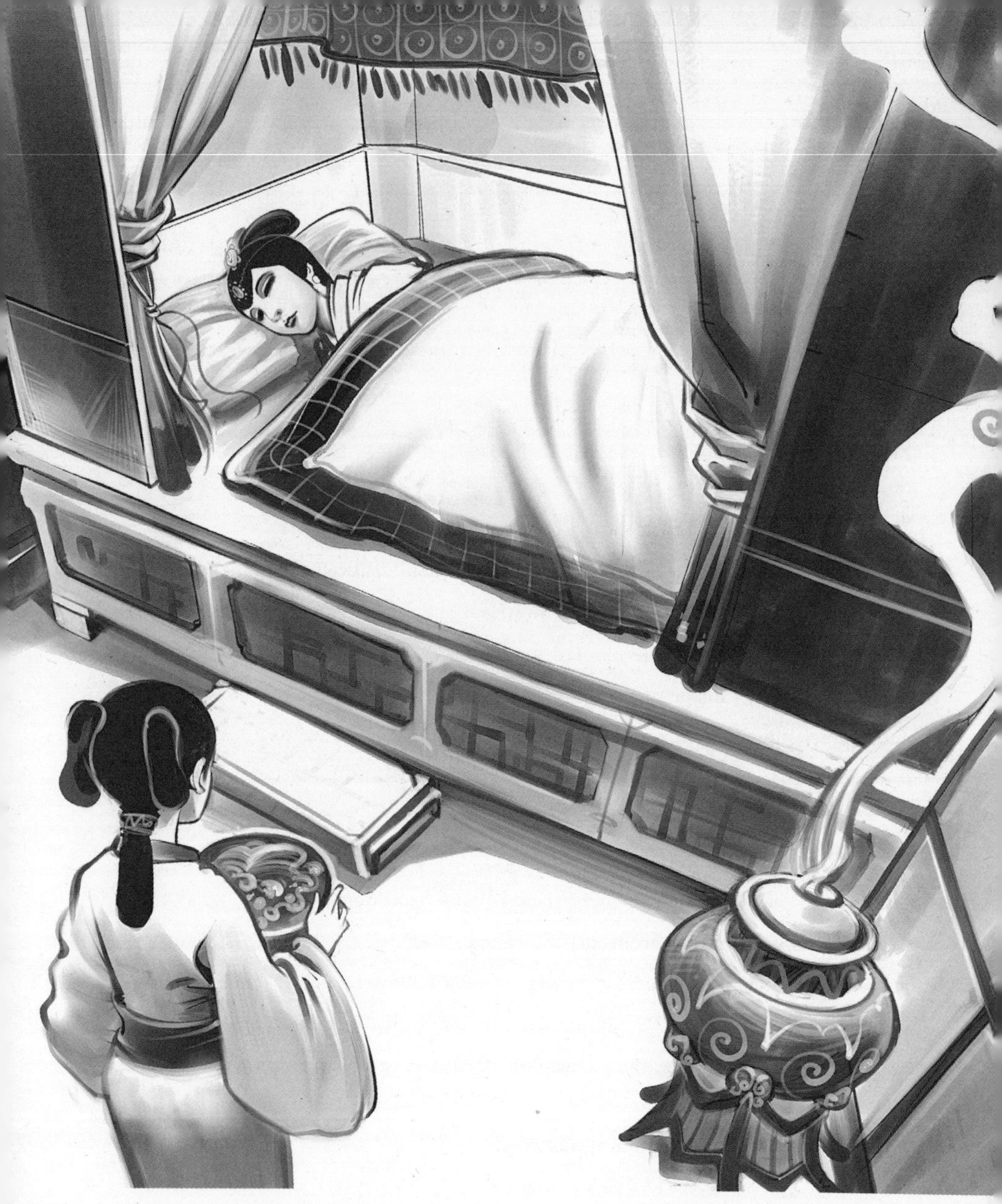

没过多久，丽娘一病不起。杜宝夫妇心急如焚，四处寻找名医，给女儿看病，可是求医问卜，总不见效，丽娘的病越来越重了。

这天晚上是中秋佳节，连绵的秋雨终于停了下来。丽娘躺在榻上，吩咐春香打开窗户，晚风拂面，明月高悬，银光流泻，小小的绣房也变得晶莹剔透起来。丽娘见月色如此美丽，便挣扎着从绣榻上坐了起来，春香连忙过去扶她。丽娘想起自从梦见书生，自己就得了心病，恐怕是无药可医了，想到这里，她的内心一阵疼痛，猛烈地咳嗽了几声。春香生怕丽娘过度伤心，连忙柔声劝慰。

Before long, Du Liniang was confined to her bed with a serious illness. Burning with anxiety, Du Bao and Lady Du had many famous doctors come to see her and consulted oracles, but none produced the desired result. Du Liniang went from bad to worse.

It was the Mid-autumn Festival, and at last the uninterrupted autumn rain came to an end. Du Liniang was lying on her couch. She told Chunxiang to open the windows. A night breeze came over lightly. A full moon hung high above in the sky and moonlight streamed down bright, making her bedroom glittering and translucent. Enchanted by the beauty of the moonlight, Du Liniang struggled to sit up on the bed. Chunxiang rushed over to support her. Du Liniang thought, “I fell sick since I dreamed of the young scholar, and I don’t have any hope of getting recovered.” As she thought of this, she was struck with a fit of pain in the heart, which sent her to a violent burst of coughs. Fearing that her mistress might be excessively grief-stricken, Chunxiang consoled her with encouraging words in a soft voice.

漫漫长夜，雁叫声声，草间的虫鸣，和着风吹窗棂声一起袭来。丽娘坐在绣榻上，只觉得风寒透骨，全身微颤，突然一阵惊悸，向后一倒，不省人事。春香惊慌失措，连忙大声呼喊，甄氏闻声赶来，她看到女儿奄奄一息的样子，便痛哭不止。

丽娘从昏迷中清醒过来，看见母亲正靠在绣榻前，她挣扎着要春香搀扶自己，颤巍巍地对着母亲拜了两拜，哭道："母亲，不孝的女儿拜谢您的养育之恩了。"甄氏心如刀割，一把抱住女儿。丽娘虚弱地说道："母亲，这后花园中有一棵梅树，是我平生最爱。女儿死了之后，请母亲将我葬于梅树之下。"

The night seemed endless. The cries of the wild geese and the insects in the grass, accompanied by the rattling of the window lattices in the wind, stole into Du Liniang's bedroom. As she was sitting on the couch, Du Liniang suddenly felt the icy wind penetrated to the very bones. With a shiver, she fell backward and went into a coma. Chunxiang panicked at this sight and shouted aloud for help. Lady Du rushed over and started to wail bitterly as she found that her daughter was at her last gasp.

When she came to her senses, Du Liniang found her mother was at her couch and bade Chunxiang to help her up. Falling on her knees and shaking all over, she performed two bows towards Lady Du and said, "Mother, I, your unfilial daughter, thank you for all your trouble and care!" Heart-broken, Lady Du pulled Du Liniang into her arms. Du Liniang continued in a feeble voice, "Mother, in the back garden there is a plum tree that I love best. Please bury me under that tree after I die."

丽娘又叫过春香，吩咐道：“春香，我死之后，你要好好侍奉老爷和夫人。”说到这里，又喘息了一阵，说道：“我那幅春容画像，千万不要让外人看见，你用个紫檀匣子，把它藏到太湖石底下。”春香一边流泪一边点头答应着。

哭声终于惊动了杜宝，他匆匆赶来，看到女儿如此情形，和甄氏抱头痛哭。丽娘的身体渐渐不支，躺在绣榻上对父亲说道：“爹爹，今夜是中秋了吧？”杜宝哽咽着应了一声。丽娘长叹一声道：“唉，什么时候还能重见这月色……”她的气息越来越微弱，永远闭上了眼睛。

Du Liniang then asked Chunxiang to move closer to her and said, “Chunxiang, look after my parents after I die.” Having said this, Du Liniang gasped for a while and continued, “I’ve thought of another thing, my portrait. Don’t let strangers see it. Put it in a red sandalwood case and bury it beneath the Taihu rocks after I die.” Tears came to Chunxiang’s eyes as she nodded her consent.

Hearing the sobs, Du Bao came to Du Liniang’s bedroom in a rush. At the sight of his daughter, he and his wife cried bitterly on each other’s shoulder. Du Liniang was going from worse to worst. Lying in her bed, she said to her father, “Father, is tonight the Mid-autumn Festival?” Du Bao nodded, choking with sobs. Heaving a sigh, Du Liniang said, “Ah, when shall I have the chance to see this moonlight again…” Her breathing became fainter and fainter and finally she breathed her last.

杜宝夫妻肝肠寸断，痛不欲生，春香也哭得很伤心。他们按照丽娘的临终遗言，将她埋葬在梅树下面，那幅画像被春香藏在了太湖石底。杜宝为了纪念女儿，在花园旁盖起一座庵堂，起名“梅花观”，安置丽娘神位。

丧事刚料理完毕，杜宝便接到朝廷的旨令。原来金兵南侵，朝廷提升杜宝为安抚使，命他立即镇守淮扬。杜宝只好叮嘱陈最良和一个姓石的道姑看守丽娘神位，自己带着夫人、春香匆匆赴任去了。

Du Bao and his wife were tormented and torn apart with grief. Chunxiang was also overwhelmed with sadness. In accordance with Du Liniang's last words, they buried her under the plum tree. Chunxiang hid the portrait of Du Liniang beneath the Taihu rocks. In memory of his daughter, Du Bao had a nunnery built by the garden and named it the Plum Blossom Nunnery to keep his daughter's memorial tablet.

No sooner had Du Bao arranged his daughter's funeral then he received the imperial edict. On account of the Jin's southward intrusion, Du Bao was promoted to the Envoy of Appeasement in charge of the affairs in Huaiyang and was ordered to commence the transference without delay. Du Bao asked Chen Zuiliang and Mother Stone, a nun, to watch over the memorial tablet of Du Liniang. With that, Du Bao, along with his wife and Chunxiang, set off for his new post.

转眼三年过去了，陈最良在杜小姐死后，找不到教书的地方，生活非常贫困。眼看已是隆冬季节了，北风呼啸，大雪纷飞，陈最良出门拜访朋友，在雪地里救起一个进京赶考的书生。

这书生姓柳名梦梅，是唐朝文学家柳宗元的后代，家住岭南，从小父母双亡，生活艰难，此番进京赶考，还是得到朋友资助的路费才成行的。好不容易走到这南安府，寒冬腊月，衣衫单薄，患了风寒，腿脚一软，便摔倒在雪地里了。

陈最良见这书生病体虚弱，动了恻隐之心，便将他扶到梅花观里，暂时住了下来。

In the twinkling of the eye, three years passed. As Chen Zuiliang failed to find a teaching job to earn a living after Du Liniang's death, he had lived in poverty. Deep winter was drawing near. It was a windy and snowy day. While Chen Zuiliang was on a visit to a friend, he rescued a young scholar from the snow who was on his way to the capital for the highest imperial examination.

This young scholar was called Liu Mengmei, a descendant of the well-known Tang Dynasty writer Liu Zongyuan. A native of the South of the Five Ridges, he lost his parents when he was very young and had lived a very difficult life ever since. It was the financial aid of a friend that made his trip to the capital for the highest imperial examination possible. When he finally made it to Nan'an, it was cold winter. He caught a cold for lack of clothes. Getting weak in the knees, he fell on the snowy ground.

Seeing this weak and sick young man, Chen Zuiliang felt sorry for him and helped him to the Plum Blossom Nunnery to put him up for the time being.

转眼冬去春来，柳梦梅病体渐渐痊愈。这天他忽然觉得心中烦闷，难以排遣，打算出去散心。石道姑告诉他，后面有一座花园，景致不错。

柳梦梅别了石道姑，独自漫步到园中，只见园里满目荒凉，院墙半倒，杂草丛生。一湾清澈的溪水，潺潺流淌，溪边的亭台经过风吹雨打，已经黯然失色了。树下那一架秋千，无比寂寞地在微风中摇曳。柳梦梅心想，一个女道士住的梅花观，怎么会有这么大一座花园呢？这里没有经历兵火，怎么这般凄凉？

Soon spring arrived and Liu Mengmei got much better. One day, he felt somewhat bored and depressed and wished to go somewhere to have some fun. Mother Stone suggested that the garden behind the Nunnery was a good place for a visit.

After saying goodbye to Mother Stone, Liu Mengmei set out for the garden on foot. Arriving at the garden, a scene of desolation met his eyes. Some walls had tumbled down and the whole garden was overgrown with tall weeds. A limpid brook was flowing there like a piece of beautiful music. The pavilion by the brook was overshadowed due to exposure to wind and rain. The swing under the tree swayed in the breeze desolately. “How come there is such a large garden in this Plum Blossom Nunnery?” Liu Mengmei wondered. “It was not molested by war or fire. What has turned it into such a ruined state?”

他一边走一边思索着，只见前面出现了一丛太湖山石堆砌的假山，他来到湖山石畔，坐下来休息了片刻。正准备起身，突然发现身后有一个小小山洞，他凑过去，看见洞里藏着一个檀木匣子。

柳梦梅非常惊讶，打开匣子，只见里面有一幅画，他饶有兴致地展开画卷，原来是一幅观音的画像。他笑了笑，心想，这观音独自在此，肯定寂寞，不如将画像带回观中供着，每天顶礼膜拜，也体现我的一片虔诚之心。想罢，便小心翼翼地捧着匣子回观中去了。

He pondered as he walked on. Soon he saw a rockwork piled up with Taihu rocks. He came to the rockwork, sat down and rested for a while. As he was about to get onto his feet, he suddenly noticed a small cavern. Getting closer to the cavern, he found a red sandalwood case hidden there.

Very much surprised, Liu Mengmei opened the sandal case and found there was a scroll painting. He unfolded the scroll curiously. It was a portrait of benevolent Guanyin. He thought to himself, smiling, “This Guanyin must feel lonely. Why don’t I bring it back to my room and pay homage to her every day. It will be much better than having it buried there, and also it will give me a chance to show my sincerity.” So thinking, he took the case very cautiously to the Nunnery.

回到观中，他打开匣子，细细欣赏起这幅观音画像来。只见画中的观音皎洁美丽，像月中的嫦娥一样妩媚多姿。可是为什么这观音穿的裙子下面，还露出一双小脚呢？柳梦梅满腹狐疑。他想，难道是嫦娥的画像？可是这嫦娥身边没有半点祥云衬托，画中的那棵树也不像是月中桂树。

他看来看去，觉得画中人倒像一位人间女子，一位思春的大家闺秀。画像上还题着一首诗，最后一句，“不在梅边在柳边”，这不是把自己的姓和名都写进去了么？

When he was back to the Nunnery, Liu Mengmei opened the case, spread the scroll and started to appreciate it. Charming and pretty, the Guanyin in the portrait was like Chang'er in the moon. “But why does the skirt of this Guanyin disclose a pair of tiny feet?” Liu Mengmei became a little bit suspicious. “Could it be a portrait of Chang'er? But if it were Chang'er, why isn't she accompanied by rosy clouds? What's more, the tree in the scroll is not like the laurel tree on the moon.”

He examined it more closely and found it was more like a portrait of a human, a fair young girl. There was also a poem in the top corner, and the last line read, “It must be by a willow instead of a plum.” He wondered, “Why is it the words in this line contain my name Liu (willow) Mengmei (plum)?”

只见画中的美人，哀愁淡淡，娴雅婀娜，一双美目，秋波流转，含情脉脉，她手中捻着半枝青梅，好像要对自己诉说什么。柳梦梅看着看着，不觉如痴如醉地喊道："美人！美人！姐姐！姐姐！"他恨不得插上翅膀，飞到画幅中去。想着想着，便迷迷糊糊地进入了梦乡。

一阵敲门声使他猛地惊醒过来。窗外风声飒飒，翠竹摇曳，柳梦梅问道："是风是人？"窗外响起一个女子清脆的嗓音："有人。"柳梦梅想，肯定是石道姑给自己送茶水来了，他起身开门，不禁"啊呀"一声，惊得目瞪口呆。

The beautiful girl in the scroll painting, wearing a faint woe on the face though, appeared to be pretty graceful for a pair of eloquent eyes and tender affections. Holding a plum in the hand, it looked like she wanted to say something to Liu Mengmei. As he stared at the painted beauty, Liu Mengmei cried involuntarily, totally intoxicated, "My beauty! My beauty! My sister! My sister!" He wished he could have wings and fly into the painting. As his thoughts wandered, he dozed off into a dreamland.

A burst of knocks on the door suddenly awakened him. The wind outside of the window was whistling and the bamboo leaves were rustling. "Is it the wind or someone there?" Liu Mengmei asked. "It's me," came a reply from outside. Liu Mengmei thought, "It must be Stone Mother bringing me tea." He rose to his feet and opened the door. "Ouch!" he couldn't refrain from letting out a cry, stunned and speechless.

月光下站着一个亭亭玉立的少女，面庞皎洁，光彩照人。那女子闪身进门，对着柳梦梅行礼道："秀才万福。"柳梦梅如梦初醒，连忙关上房门，问道："你是谁家女子？为何深夜到此？"那女子嫣然一笑，答道："秀才，你猜。"柳梦梅无奈，只好猜道："你是天上的仙女？还是从大户人家逃出来的姬妾？或者是夜里赶路，来我这里借灯的？"那女子摇摇头，神秘地笑道："我是东邻的女孩子，特意来和你说说话的。"柳梦梅又问道："你家里还有什么人？"

Under the moonlight, Liu Mengmei saw a slim and graceful girl standing right before him. The girl slipped into his room and greeted him, "Boundless happiness to you, Mr. Scholar!" As if wakening from a dream, Liu Mengmei hurriedly shut the door and said, "May I ask where Your Ladyship is from? And what brings you here at such an hour of the night?" Smiling, the girl said, "Mr. Scholar, you can make a guess." Having no choice, Liu Mengmei guessed, "You might be a fairy maiden? Or you're a concubine from a rich and influential family trying to get yourself out of your husband's confinement? Or you must have lost your way in the dark and have to go to my room to borrow a candle?" Shaking her head, the girl said, "I'm your next door neighbor and I'm especially here to have a few words with you." Liu Mengmei further asked, "Who is there in your family?"

[redacted]

那女子沉默了片刻，答道："斜阳外，芳草涯，再无人有伶仃的爹妈。奴年二八，没包弹风藏叶里花。为春归惹动嗟呀，瞥见你风神俊雅。无他，待和你剪烛临风，西窗闲话。"①

柳梦梅似懂非懂，傻傻说道："美人半夜来到我这里，大概是梦吧！"那女子羞涩地笑道："不是梦，我还怕秀才不肯接纳我呢。"柳梦梅听到这话，忙答道："能得到美人垂青，小生喜出望外，怎么敢推辞呢？"那女子凝视着他的脸，意味深长地叹道："我真的盼到你了！"

After a moment of silence, the girl said, "West of the setting sun, at a remote place, I reside with my aged parents. I'm sixteen and a bud sheltered by patron leaves. The ebbing spring had evoked in me a woe and that's why I caught sight of your face. I come here for no other purpose but to keep you company during the lengthy nights."

Somewhat suspicious about what she said, Liu Mengmei continued, "A beauty has come to me at midnight. Could our meeting be a dream?" "No, this is no dream," replied the girl. "I was wondering if you would accept me." Hearing this, Liu Mengmei responded hurriedly, "If you mean it, I will be the happiest man in the world. In no way I'm going to turn you down." Looking into Liu Mengmei's eyes, the girl said meaningfully, "At last, now my dream has come true!"

① 这支曲子的大意是：我住在夕阳下，芳草地里，孤苦伶仃，我十六岁，就像藏在叶子里的鲜花一样。我正在为春天的归去叹息，突然看到你这个风流英俊的人。我来这里没有别的事，就是想和你坐在西窗下，对着烛光说话。

二人坐下畅谈，说得非常开心。柳梦梅见她笑语盈盈，娇羞默默，不由心神摇荡，他大胆走上前去，握住那女子的手，一把将她抱在怀里。那女子起初非常害羞，后来也就半推半就，二人彻夜未眠。

那女子郑重地叮咛道："妾千金之躯，一旦付与郎君，勿负奴心。"柳梦梅连忙起誓，又问道："请问姐姐贵姓芳名？"那女子的眼里闪过一丝阴影，答道："我是正经人家的女儿，怕说出姓名来招惹是非。"柳梦梅也不好再问。从此，这女子暮来朝去，两人情投意合，十分恩爱。

They sat down and started to talk on and on without inhibition and both were very happy. Liu Mengmei was very much captured by her smiles and loveliness. Picking up his courage, he moved over and caught her by the hand and pulled her into his arms. At first the girl felt a bit shy, but in the end she yielded to him with just a show of reluctance. Then they enjoyed merrymaking all night.

The girl said in a serious tone, "I've given my heart and soul to you. Do not abuse my love." Liu Mengmei swore he would never let her down. Then he asked further, "May I know you of your name?" "I'm the daughter of a decent family," she said, "I have fears that gossips may arise and spread if I disclose my name." Hearing this, Liu made no further enquiries. From then on, the girl kept on coming to date Liu Mengmei at night and leaving his room at daybreak. Both found one another congenial and loved each other heart and soul.

世上没有不透风的墙，这事竟被庙里的石道姑知道了。这天晚上，柳梦梅和这女子正在喝酒赏月，忽然，门“吱呀”一声开了，石道姑闯了进来。柳梦梅顿时手足无措，正准备用身子遮挡那女子，哪知转身一看，那女子早就不见了。

石道姑来到那幅画像面前，自言自语道：“刚才分明看见一个女子的身影，怎么到了跟前就变成了画像？难道真的有鬼么？”她问道：“秀才，你每天晚上在这房里唧唧咕咕，到底是和谁在说话？”柳梦梅见她没有看到那女子，放下心来，答道：“唉，老姑姑，我是在对着这画上的观音祈福呢。”

As the saying goes, walls have ears. Stone Mother learned all about the affair happened to Liu Mengmei. One night while Liu Mengmei and the girl were drinking wine and enjoying the glorious full moon, the door opened and in came Stone Mother. Immediately Liu Mengmei was at a loss as to what to do. As he turned around and was about to shield the girl, he found the girl was nowhere to be seen.

Getting closer to the scroll painting, Mother Stone thought aloud, “I did see a shadow of a girl just now with my own eyes. How come I should only see a portrait on the wall? Could it have a spirit of its own?” Turning to Liu Mengmei, Mother Stone asked, “Young Schoar, I heard you murmur in your room at night many times. Who was it you were speaking to?” Feeling much relieved as he found Mother Stone didn’t see the girl, Liu Mengmei answered, “Oh, Mother Stone, I was praying to this portrait of Guanyin so that she could protect me.”

石道姑走后，柳梦梅掀起画幅，那女子早已无影无踪了，他心里沉吟道："这美人藏到哪里了呢？怎么脚步这样轻？难道真是天上的仙女不成？"他心中无限狐疑。

第二天晚上，那女子又飘然而至，柳梦梅便道："姐姐昨晚受惊了！"那女子轻轻笑了笑，并不在意，两人又饶有兴致地交谈起来，当柳梦梅提出要去拜见那个女子的父母时，她的脸上便显出了疑难之色，说道："你到我家去，只能见我，要见我的父母还早。"柳梦梅愕然问道："为什么？难道你真的是天仙吗？"

After Mother Stone was gone, Liu Mengmei lifted up the scroll and found the girl had vanished into thin air. "Where has my beauty gone?" he muttered to himself. "Why are her footsteps so light? Could it really possible she is a fairy maid?" He was filled with suspicion.

The following night the girl arrived as usual. Liu Mengmei said to her, "You must have been frightened last night!" Smiling softly, the girl appeared as if she didn't care much about what had happened the previous night. Immediately they started chatting with interest. As Liu Mengmei proposed to pay a visit to the girls' parents, the girl gave a pained look. "If you come," said the girl, "you'll only be able to meet myself. It's still too soon to meet my parents." "Why?" Liu Mengmei asked, astounded. "Could it be possible that you're really a celestial being?"

柳梦梅又说道：“看你总是独来独往，连个姓名也不肯透露，一定是天仙了，我可消受不起，老天爷会责罚的。”那女子

连忙分辩。柳梦梅道："姐姐，你这也不肯说，那也不肯说，难道你真是私奔之女、花月之妖？"那女子欲言又止，叹口气道："我想说，可是怎么出口呢？秀才，你先和我对天盟誓，结为夫妻，我再说。"

柳梦梅一听，马上拉了那女子，拈香盟誓道："神天的，神天的，盟香满爇。柳梦梅，柳梦梅，南安郡舍。遇了这佳人提挈作夫妻，生同室，死同穴。口不心齐，寿随香灭。"

"You walk in the depth of night without the attendance of a maid," Liu Mengmei continued. "Since you refuse to tell me your name, you must be a celestial being. I'm afraid I'm too humble to deserve your love, otherwise it will be hard for me to evade heavenly punishment." The girl tried to offer an explanation in a hurry. Liu Mengmei added, "Sister, it seems that you're reluctant to tell me more about who you are. Could you be a run-away girl or a spirit of a flower?" The girl wished to speak but stopped on a second thought. Letting out a deep sigh, she said, "I want to tell, but how should I say it? Mr. Scholar, I'll tell you when a vow is made. You take an oath that you make me your first and only wife, and then I'll tell you."

Upon hearing this, Liu Mengmei immediately took the girl by the hand, lit the incense and vowed, "Heaven above, the incense proves my words. I am Liu Mengmei, sojourning in Nan'an. This beauty by my side bestows me with her love and we have decided to be husband and wife. While we live, we shall live under one roof. When we die, we shall lie in the same grave. If I go against this vow, I will expire with this burning incense stick."

听到这里，那女子不禁潸然泪下。柳梦梅问道："小姐怎么掉下泪来？"那女子抹泪叹道："你的款款深情，真让我感动。"说罢迟疑了一下，像是话到嘴边又咽了回去，最后，她才开口说道："秀才，你知道吗？我是南安杜太守的女儿，小名丽娘，我就是这画中人。"柳梦梅讶然道："呀！原来是杜安抚的千金小姐！"没想到那女子接口道："秀才，奴家还不是人。""不是人？难道是鬼？"那女子流泪道："是鬼。"

Tears trickled down the girl's face as she heard Liu Mengmei's vow. "Why are you crying, Miss?" Heaving a sigh, the girl answered, "Your words have really touched my heart." Having said this, the girl hesitated for a moment as if her words were stopped in the throat. Finally, she spoke again, "Mr. Scholar, I'm the daughter of the former Magistrate of Nan'an. My name is Du Liniang and I'm the very girl painted on this painting." Surprised, Liu Mengmei said, "So you're the daughter of the Magistrate Du of Nan'an!" "I'm not a mortal one yet," the girl interrupted him. "Not a mortal one? Are you a ghost?" asked Liu Mengmei. "Yes, I am a ghost," said the girl.

柳梦梅顿时觉得一股阴气扑面而来，毛骨悚然，心中不免有几分害怕，战战兢兢地说道："你真的是鬼？真的？"那女子含泪答道："是的，我是杜太守家死去的女儿杜丽娘。"柳梦梅看着杜丽娘，说道："你是我的妻子，即使是鬼我也不害怕了。请问小姐，这究竟是怎么一回事？你怎么能够回到阳世来与我见面？"

杜丽娘长叹一声，坐在柳梦梅身边，将自己梦中与折柳秀才相会，因梦成痴，一病不起，伤情而死，但死后孤魂不散，又判为还阳复活之事一一告诉了柳梦梅。

Liu Mengmei suddenly felt a surge of chilly air blowing against his face, making him feel terrified. Afraid and trembling, Liu Mengmei asked, "Are you really a ghost? Is this true?" "Yes," the girl answered with tears in her eyes. "I'm Du Liniang, Magistrate Du's dead daughter." Fixing his eyes on Du Liniang, Liu Mengmei said, "Now that you're my wife, I'm no longer afraid of you even though you're a ghost. But Miss, could you tell me the whole story? How are you going to come back this world to meet with me?"

Heaving a long sigh, the girl sat beside Liu Mengmei and, one after another, told him how she had dreamed of Scholar Liu, how she had fallen ill and never recovered and died of grief, how her spirit had been hanging on around, and how she had been granted permission to resurrect by the nether judge.

原来，杜丽娘死后，魂魄来到地府，判官判她阳寿未尽，与父母还有重会之时，并查了姻缘簿，告诉她有一个叫柳梦梅的书生，与她有夫妻之缘，因此特意放她的魂魄出来，随风游荡，寻找这个书生。

那天晚上她来到梅花观中，看到厢房里站着一个书生，对着一幅画像在呼唤。她凑过去一看，原来正是自己生前描绘的那幅春容，而这个深情款款的书生，竟与自己的梦中情人长得一模一样！她的鬼魂飘进那书生的房间，只见自己的画像下有一首和诗，署名是岭南柳梦梅。

It turned out that when Du Liniang's spirit arrived at the nether world after her death, the nether judge decided that she still had more years to live and still had the chance to meet her parents. The nether judge consulted the Marriage Book and told her that there would be a young scholar by the name of Liu Mengmei who would be destined to be her husband. The nether judge let go of her spirit so that she could flutter with the wind and look for Liu Mengmei.

One night she came to the Plum Blossom Nunnery and sighted that a young scholar was standing there in a wing-room and talking to a portrait. Moving closer, she found that the portrait was none other than the painting she had painted when she was alive and the young man none other than the man she had met in her dream! Her spirit fluttered into the young man's room and found a poem in the lower corner of the painting written in the same rhyme with hers. The signature of the poem was Liu Mengmei from the South of the Five Ridges.

杜丽娘不禁百感交集，经历千辛万苦，终于盼来了自己的心上人。她回去禀告了冥府判官，决定趁此良宵，与柳梦梅完成夙愿。于是她现出人形，半夜敲窗，与柳梦梅相见并以身相许，结成夫妇。她不敢把自己的身世说出来，只好托言说自己是邻家的女孩儿。

她告诉柳梦梅如今自己的阴数已尽，只要柳梦梅亲自掘开梅树下的坟墓，自己便可以还魂复生。她希望柳梦梅能够救她回到阳间，并叮咛道："你我已结为夫妻，愿你能救我重回阳世。我若不得复生，在九泉之下必会痛恨你！"

All kinds of feeling welled up in Du Liniang's heart. After experiencing innumerable trials and hardships, she had finally run into her sweetheart. She went back and told the nether judge about her adventure. She decided to take that beautiful night to fulfill her long-cherished wish of meeting Liu Mengmei. Then taking on a human form and knocking at Liu Mengmei's door at midnight, she met with Liu Mengmei and pledged to marry him. As she found it quite improper to tell Liu Mengmei her true origin, she had to tell him that she was just the daughter of a next-door neighbor.

Also she told Liu Mengmei that her days in the nether world had come to an end and she would revive from death if Liu Mengmei personally unearthed her from the tomb under the plum tree. She earnestly hoped that Liu Mengmei could bring her back to the sunny world. She urged again and again, "Since you've made me your wife, please help me to come back to the sunny world. If I can't return to life, I'll loathe you even in the nether world!"

柳梦梅如梦初醒，好半天才回过神来，杜丽娘的鬼魂已经飘走了。柳梦梅被杜丽娘的深情感动得整晚都没有睡着，他决定明天就去找观里的石道姑商量，掘坟开棺，迎接杜小姐回生。

第二天清早，他把这事的经过一五一十地告诉了石道姑，石道姑惊讶了半天，以为是柳梦梅撞见鬼了，始终不肯相信。最后还是杜小姐鬼魂显灵，石道姑才相信了柳梦梅的话。她叫自己的侄儿前来帮忙，为杜小姐开棺。

It was quite some time before Liu Mengmei, as if wakening from a dream, recovered his senses. By then Du Liniang's spirit has already floated away. Moved by Du Liniang's deep feelings, Liu Mengmei kept awake all night long. He decided to go and talk it over with Mother Stone to seek her advice on excavating the grave and opening the coffin and bringing Miss Du back to life.

The next morning, Liu Mengmei told Mother Stone in full detail what had happened to him. Startled by Liu Mengmei's story, Mother Stone did not believing a word of it, thinking that he must have been possessed. Finally, the presence of Miss Du's spirit made Mother Stone believe Liu Mengmei's words. Then Mother Stone told her nephew to come over and give a hand in excavating Miss Du's grave.

GABRIEL

三人走进后花园，只见半亭瓦砾，满地荆棘，柳梦梅不禁叹了一口气，比起春天，这里更显得荒凉冷落了，一切依稀如梦幻般。石道姑看出柳梦梅心情焦虑，便劝道："秀才不要心急，杜小姐的孤坟，就在这梅树下。"说罢三人就动手挖了起来。

不久，便见到黄土中露出了一副小小的棺材，柳梦梅连忙叮嘱道："小心！"只听见棺中传来"哎哟"一声，正是女子娇柔清脆的嗓音，柳梦梅连忙挽起衣袖，和石道姑一起，小心翼翼地挪开了棺盖。

They three got to the Back Garden. All they saw was half a pavilion in rubble and a ground overspread with thorn and bramble. Liu Mengmei could not refrain from letting out a deep sigh. Unlike the springtime, the Back Garden appeared more bleak and desolate and everything was as hazy as a long perished dream. Liu Mengmei was anxious, Mother Stone advised him, "Young Scholar, don't be impatient. Miss Du's grave is right over there under the plum tree." So saying, they three got to the mound and started digging.

Before long, a tiny coffin was revealed from under the yellow earth. Liu Mengmei urged again and again, "Be careful!" Then a sound "Ouch" came from within the coffin. It was the voice of a girl, clear and melodious. Rolling up his sleeves, Liu Mengmei, with the help of Mother Stone, moved away the cover of the coffin with great care.

一股异香扑面而来，一个年轻女子闭着眼睛躺在棺材里，面色若生，如花似玉，正是杜小姐。

柳梦梅轻轻扶起杜小姐，只见她的眼睛缓缓睁开。柳梦梅心花怒放，连忙将她扶到牡丹亭上，石道姑倒了一杯热酒给她。杜丽娘渐渐清醒过来，开口道："哪个是柳郎？"柳梦梅连忙答应，丽娘含泪说道："柳郎重生之恩，胜过亲生父母。"二人脉脉含情，对视良久。

柳梦梅怕丽娘身体柔弱不堪风吹，便将她扶到梅花观中，卧床将息。

A pleasant, balmy smell burst out. A young girl, as pretty as a flower, was there lying in the coffin, her eyes closed. Her complexion was not a bit changed. She was no other than Miss Du.

Liu Mengmei brought Miss Du to her feet with care and Miss Du opened her eyes slowly. Greatly elated, Liu Mengmei assisted her to the Peony Pavilion at once. Mother Stone poured a cup of warm wine into Miss Du's mouth. Coming back to life, Du Liniang said, "Which of you is Scholar Liu?" "I am Liu Mengmei," Liu Mengmei answered promptly. With tears in her eyes, Du Liniang continued, "You give me my second chance to live. I owe you more than my own parents." They looked at each other for quite a long time.

Fearing that Du Liniang might not be strong enough to stand the wind, Liu Mengmei assisted her to the Plum Blossom Nunnery to take a rest.

经过一段时间的精心调养，丽娘的身体渐渐恢复了。这天她正和柳梦梅在房中谈心，忽然响起了急促的敲门声，原来是陈最良前来探望柳梦梅。丽娘赶紧躲了起来。

陈最良对柳梦梅说道："我准备了一个礼盒，特来邀请柳兄明日一道去给杜小姐上坟。"柳梦梅听了心中一惊，只好勉强答应，把陈最良打发走了。

After a period of recuperation, Du Liniang was nursed back to health. One day, there suddenly came a pressing knocking on the gate while she and Liu Mengmei were chatting in the room. It was Chen Zuiliang paying a visit to Liu Mengmei. Du Lininag hid herself in haste.

Chen Zuiliang said to Liu Mengmei, "I've prepared a basket of food, and I would like to invite you for an excursion to Miss Du's tomb at noontime tomorrow." Taken by surprise, Liu Mengmei had no other choice but to give his consent, and then Chen Zuiliang left.

石道姑说道：“这事若被陈最良知道，麻烦就大了。他不会相信小姐复活的，说不定还会说小姐是妖怪。”

“老姑姑，那怎么办才好呢？”柳梦梅问道。“只有一个办法，”石道姑说道，“柳秀才要去临安赶考，不如你们结成夫妻，找一只船，连夜走，神不知鬼不觉。不知二位意下如何？”杜柳二人别无他计，只好如此。

石道姑找出一壶酒，说道：“如今也顾不得许多了，有酒在此，你二人赶紧拜天地罢。”于是他们拜石道姑为媒人，并在她的主持下，手捧酒杯，双膝下跪，拜天地，正式结为夫妻。

Mother Stone said, “We would get into trouble if Chen Zuiliang learned about all this. He will never believe that Miss Du would come back to life. Worse still, he might insist that Miss Du is an evil spirit.”

“What shall we do, Old Mother?” asked Liu Mengmei. “There is only one way out,” said Mother Stone. “Miss Du, since Liu Mengmei is on his way to Lin’an for the imperial examination, why don’t you put up with a simple wedding? Then you can find a boat, slip away in the dead of the night so that there will be no trace left. What do you think of this idea?” As they had not got a better idea, Du and Liu had to let it be so.

Finding out a flask of wine, Mother Stone said, “Now we don’t have the time for formalities. I’ve got some wine here, and now you may kowtow to heaven and earth.” Then, taking Mother Stone as their matchmaker, Du and Liu each held up a cup of wine, fell on their knees, kowtowed to heaven and earth and became man and wife in due form.

石道姑又匆匆找来一艘船，三人连夜上路，离开南安府前往临安。路上一帆风顺，不几日便来到了临安，柳梦梅在郊外租了一所空房，将丽娘和石道姑安顿下来。自己也开始临窗苦读，准备即将到来的科举考试。

这天，他正在后堂和丽娘闲话，只见石道姑提着一壶酒匆匆赶回，说道："相公，小姐，我看见各处秀才都赴考场去了，相公快走，别错过了好事。"柳梦梅一听就忙乱起来，他喝了丽娘递过来的状元红，又叮嘱丽娘好好在家等待消息，便匆匆忙忙赶赴考场去了。

Mother Stone got a boat in haste and they three set off the same night, leaving Nan'an for Lin'an. It was a plain sailing and they arrived in Lin'an in a few days. Liu Mengmei rented a vacant house in the outskirts and had Du Liniang and Mother Stone settled up. Meanwhile Liu Mengmei started to study hard to prepare for the forthcoming imperial examination.

One day, while Liu and Du were chatting in the room, Mother Stone came to them in a flurry, holding a wind flask, and said, "Master and Mistress, I saw scholars from every part of the country hurrying to the examination court. You'd better hurry too. Don't miss a golden chance." This threw Liu Mengmei into a rush and a muddle. He drank up the Red Zhuangyuan wine Du Liniang gave him and repeatedly advised her to be patient and wait for his good news. Then he headed for the examination court in a rush.

来到考场，考试已经结束了。守门的小卒不让他进去。柳梦梅傻傻地嚷道："我说不定是个状元呢，你快让我进去！"喊声惊动了主考官苗舜宾，他见这个秀才胸有成竹的样子，便允许他重新补考。不久，柳梦梅就交了卷。

苗舜宾一看柳梦梅的文章，见解高明，寥寥数句，胜过千言万语，心中大喜，想道：真是国家的栋梁之才啊，幸好没有错过。他吩咐柳梦梅等候发榜。自己便进宫去了。

哪想到这时候边报紧急，大金国派李全为先锋，正向淮扬一带大举进犯。皇上正在为此事发愁，无心阅读苗舜宾呈上来的卷子，发榜的事因此耽搁了下来。

When Liu Mengmei arrived at the examination court, the examination had been over. As the guard on duty refused his request to go into the examination court, Liu Mengmei started shouting, "Maybe I'll be the *zhuangyuan* left out. Let me in, please!" Liu's shouting startled Chief Examiner Miao Shunbin. Finding that this young scholar was fully prepared for the examination, Miao Shunbin admitted him the chance for a make-up exam. Before long, Liu Mengmei handed in his paper.

Miao Shunbin was overjoyed at the brilliant ideas presented in Liu Mengmei's essay after he read it. He found it much better than a thousand words though it was just a few lines. He thought to himself, "He is truly a pillar of the state. Fortunately he didn't miss the exam." Then he told Liu Mengmei to wait for the announcement of the successful candidates and then left for the imperial court.

None had expected that the frontier was now in danger. The Jin troops headed by vanguard Li Quan were invading Huaiyang. His Majesty was very much worried about this matter and was not in the mood for reading the papers Miao Shunbin submitted to him. For this reason the announcement of the successful candidates was put off.

柳梦梅回到家后，把前因后果一一告诉了丽娘，说到金兵南侵，发榜推迟，丽娘不禁想起自己远在淮扬的父母，如今正值战乱，父母生死未卜，她急得哭了起来，对柳梦梅说道："夫君，放榜时期还早，我想烦请你去淮扬打听爹娘消息，不知可否？"柳梦梅知她牵挂父母，心急如焚，只好答应下来。

但是，见了岳父岳母，如何解释丽娘还魂复生之事呢？丽娘也深知父亲生性古板执拗，不会轻易相信他的一面之词，她只好让柳梦梅把自己生前的那幅春容画带在身边，作为凭证。

After coming back to Du Liniang, Liu Mengmei told her of his experience in full detail. As he spoke of the Jin's southward invasion and the deferment of the announcement of the successful candidates, Du Liniang involuntarily thought of her parents who were then living in Huaiyang. At the time everywhere was spread with chaos caused by war. Having the least idea about her parents' life and death, Du Liniang started weeping with anxiety. She said to Liu Mengmei, "My dear husband, probably there is still some time before the ranking is announced. Do you mind making a trip to Huaiyang to seek news of my parents?" Knowing that she was very much concerned about her parents' conditions, Liu Mengmei had to comply.

How was Liu Mengmei going to explain Du Liniang's resurrection when he met his father-in-law and mother-in-law? Du Liniang was clear that her father was a pigheaded man by nature and would not easily believe Liu Mengmei's tale. So she asked Liu Mengmei to take the portrait of her with him as a proof.

就在柳梦梅赶往淮扬的同时，陈最良也在奔赴扬州的途中。杜丽娘柳梦梅二人走后的第二天清早，他备好礼盒来约柳梦梅，却见房中空空，柳梦梅和石道姑都不见了踪影。

他一个人来到后花园，又被眼前的情景吓了一大跳：只见杜小姐那高高的坟堆已经不见了，露出一个新挖的大坑，草窝里堆着棺盖，池塘里浮着一片棺木 ，料想杜小姐的尸骨已经被丢弃到池塘里去了。陈最良不禁伏地大哭，他想，这个狠心的挖坟贼不是别人，肯定就是那书生柳梦梅，真是恩将仇报啊。他急忙去南安府报了案，又星夜赶赴扬州，向杜宝夫妇报信。

While Liu Mengmei was journeying on his way to Huaiyang, Chen Zuiliang was also on a journey to Yangzhou. On the following morning after Du Liniang and Liu Mengmei left the Plum Blossom Nunnery, Chen Zuiliang came to see Liu Mengmei with a basket of food as scheduled, but found that no one was in. Liu Mengmei and Mother Stone disappeared.

As he came to the Back Garden, Chen Zuiliang was surprised at what he saw: The mound of Miss Du's tomb was no longer there and it was replaced by a big newly-dug pit. The cover of the coffin was lying in the grass and a piece of wood from the coffin was floating in the pool. He thought that Miss Du's corpse must have been thrown into the pool. He started wailing at such a terrible sight, thinking to himself, "The grave robber must be none other than that young scholar Liu Mengmei. What an ungrateful man!" He ran to the government office of Nan'an and reported it to the authorities. Then he left Nan'an for Yangzhou the same night to report this to Du Bao.

但杜宝早已不在扬州了。金将李全进犯淮扬，他的妻子杨氏却认为：扬州有杜宝镇守，难攻，不如先围了淮安，杜宝定然要

去救援，此时就可以分兵扬州，一举攻下。李全依计而行，杜宝果然率兵前去救援，临走前吩咐夫人和春香往临安避难，夫妇二人在扬州匆匆分手。

这天，杜宝正在淮安城内苦思退敌之计，只见兵士领着陈最良走了进来。他见到杜宝，二话不说，放声大哭道："老公相，夫人和春香遇害了！"杜宝大惊，问道："你如何知道？"陈最良哭道："我在贼营亲眼所见，夫人不甘凌辱，骂贼而死。"

Unfortunately, Du Bao had already been away from Yangzhou for quite some time. Lady Yang, the wife of Li Quan, the general commander of the Jin troops, counseled Li Quan when they discussed about their southward invasion, "As Yangzhou was guarded by Du Bao, it will be not easy for us to capture it. Why don't we attack Huai'an first? If we attack Huai'an, Du Bao will definitely come to its rescue. Then we can start a sudden attack on Yangzhou and capture it at our first try." Li Quan's wife's scheme worked and Du Bao really came to rescue Huai'an with his troops. Before his departure, Du Bao instructed his wife and Chunxiang to go to Lin'an to seek shelter. Thus Du Bao and his wife said goodbye in Yangzhou.

One day, while Du Bao was racking his brains for fighting against the Jin troops in the city of Huai'an, some soldiers brought Chen Zuiliang to him. At the sight of Du Bao, Chen Zuiliang started wailing and said, "My Master, Lady Du and Chunxiang were killed!" Dumbfounded, Du Bao asked, "How did you learn of this?" Chen Zuiliang said, weeping, "I saw it with my own eyes in the enemy's camp. Not willing to take humiliation, Lady Du died cursing the enemy."

原来，陈最良赶到扬州之后，得知杜宝在淮安，便转身抄小路前往淮安，没想到路上被李全的手下捉住了。李全也在苦思良策对付杜宝，他正想找一个杜宝亲信的人去淮安散布谣言，说甄氏和春香已经遇害，以乱杜宝方寸，趁机攻入淮安城。当他听说陈最良曾经做过杜宝家的塾师，不禁喜出望外，派人把陈最良领来，让士兵当着陈最良的面演了一场戏，杀了两个女人，说是甄氏和春香。然后又故意将陈最良放走，陈最良果然中计，慌慌张张奔入淮安城给杜宝送信。

It turned out that, when he got to Yangzhou, Chen Zuiliang learned that Du Bao had already gone to Huai'an. So he headed for Huai'an by taking the footpath. But he was captured by Li Quan's soldiers. At that time, Li Quan was cudgeling his brains for tactics against Du Bao. He was thinking of finding a trusted follower of Du Bao who could go and spread rumors in Huai'an saying that Lady Du and Chunxiang had been slain so as to drive Du Bao crazy with grief and take the opportunity to capture Huai'an. When he was told that Chen Zuiliang used to work as Du Bao's family tutor, Li Quan was overjoyed. Then he sent for Chen. Li Quan ordered some soldiers to put on a show of killing two women in Chen Zuiliang's presence and told him that the two women who had been killed were Lady Du and Chunxiang. Then he intentionally set Chen Zuiliang free. Chen Zuiliang really fell into the trap and rushed to the city of Huai'an in a flurry to tell Du Bao what had happened to Lady Du and Chunxiang.

杜宝肝肠寸断，不胜悲伤。陈最良又把柳梦梅伙同石道姑劫坟一事向杜宝讲述了一遍，这如同雪上加霜，杜宝心中更加痛苦无比，连连感叹道：“女儿坟墓被盗，夫人又遭难，罢了罢了！”他痛哭了一阵，又转念想到：“夫人是朝廷命妇，骂贼而死，死得壮烈。我怎能为此乱了方寸，坏了国家大事呢？”他强忍悲痛，打起精神，看着陈最良风尘仆仆的样子，忽然计上心来，他开口说道：“我这里有一件大功劳，想让先生去干，不知先生意下如何？”陈最良连忙答道：“愿意效劳。”

Du Bao was overwhelmed with grief. Then Chen Zuiliang also gave an account of Liu Mengmei and Mother Stone's violation of Miss Du's tomb, which added to his misfortunes. "My daughter's grave was violated and my wife was slain! Oh, heavens!" said Du Bao as he wept bitterly. But on second thought, he said, "My wife was a titled lady of the Court. It was entirely in character that she died cursing the enemy and died a martyr's death. I shouldn't have give way to feelings and dishearten my subordinates." Suppressing his grief and bracing himself up, Du Bao got a new idea and said to Chen Zuiliang, "I think I can give you a chance to make a name for yourself. I was wondering if you're willing to do it." "I'm at your service," answered Chen Zuiliang at once.

杜宝当下说道：“我已写好一封书信，奉劝李全，要他审时度势，倒戈投降，苦于没有找到合适的人选，老先生来得正好，麻烦你辛苦一趟。如果说得李全降顺，先生便是立了头功，老夫归奏朝廷，先生也有个为官之处。”

陈最良见是去敌营下书，心中有点害怕。杜宝安慰道：“先生不用担心，所有的事情，老夫信中已写得明明白白了，你只要把这封信交给李全的妻子杨氏，就万事大吉了。”陈最良听后谢过杜宝，抖擞精神，匆匆赶往敌营下书去了。

Du Bao said to Chen Zuiliang, “I’ve written a letter to Li Quan, demanding him to dismiss his force, but so far I haven’t been able to find a suitable messenger to deliver the letter. Would you please make a trip there? If you can persuade Li Quan into surrendering, I’ll mention your feat in my report to His Majesty, and you can be sure of acquiring an official position.”

On hearing that he was asked to deliver a letter to the enemy’s camp, Chen Zuiliang felt somewhat frightened. Du Bao consoled him, saying, “Don’t worry. I’ve had everything written explicitly in my letter. Everything will be just fine if you can deliver this letter to Li Quan’s wife.” With this, Chen Zuiliang thanked Du Bao and, bracing up his energies, hurried to the enemy’s camp to deliver the letter.

柳梦梅走后，丽娘独自在家，日日牵挂。这天夜里，她和石道姑在月下闲话，两人住在这荒村野店里，只见江声月色，星光闪烁，人迹罕至。丽娘心有所感，说到兵荒马乱中的父母和丈夫，心情显得很沉重。

一阵夜风吹过，丽娘不禁打了一个寒噤，她吩咐石道姑点灯，石道姑见灯盏中缺少灯油，便对丽娘说道："小姐你院子里坐坐，我去借点灯油来。"丽娘点点头，便独自一人坐在院子里，对着月色，聆听着江水的声音，长吁短叹。

Left alone at home since Liu Mengmei's departure, Du Liniang had been thinking of Liu Mengmei every day. It was one moonlit night resplendent with twinkling stars. Du Liniang and Mother Stone were chatting in this unfrequented small village inn. Du Liniang, due to the tumult of the war, was overcome with sadness as their digression came to her parents and husband.

Du Liniang unintentionally shivered as a gust of wind blew through. She told Mother Stone to light the lamp. Finding the lamp was short in oil, Mother Stone said to Du Liniang, "Please sit for a while in the yard, and I'll go and get some oil." Du Liniang nodded her consent and was left alone in the yard. As she listened to the babbling of the flowing river in the moonlight, she sighed and groaned, full of anxiety and grief.

院外响起了敲门声，丽娘一惊，难道是柳郎回来了？她连忙问道：“是谁？”门外有人答道：“有人借宿，行个方便。”是女子娇柔的嗓音，丽娘放了心，走过去打开院门，只见月光下站着一老一少，那少年女子挎着包袱，的确是赶路之人。丽娘连忙将她们迎进院中来。

三人在月光下打了个照面，只听见那婆婆“呀”的一声，惊讶地问道：“娘子一个人冷冷清清地坐着，怎么不点灯？”丽娘答道：“我正在赏月。”只见那婆婆好奇地瞅了她一眼，拉着那少年女子嘀咕了一句。

There came a knocking on the gate and Du Liniang was startled, thinking, “Could this be my husband Liu?” She rose to her feet and asked, “Who is it?” “We’re just passing by,” the one at the gate answered. “Can we come in?” Hearing it was the soft voice of a woman, Du Liniang felt pretty much relieved. She went over and opened the gate and found two people standing there at the gate, one was an elderly woman and the other one a young girl carrying a bundle on the arm. Seeing that they were really passer-bys, Du Liniang showed them into the yard at once.

Du Liniang and the old lady looked at each other in the face, and the old lady asked in surprise, “Miss, why do you sit here alone without a lamp?” Du Liniang answered, “I was playing with the full moon’s crystal light.” The old lady cast an inquisitively glance at Du Liniang. Then she dragged Chunxiang aside and muttered something with her.

丽娘也借着月色看了那婆婆一眼，不由大吃一惊，心中嘀咕道：“这位婆婆，怎么好像我母亲？”她回过头来问道：“敢问老夫人，从何处而来？”那婆婆长叹一声道：“从扬州来。我相公是淮扬安抚，因遭受兵难，我逃生至此。”

丽娘悲喜交集，她背过身去，流下泪来，心想：“是我母亲，我可认她？”她转过身来，那少年女子正在旁边，丽娘借着月色一看，正是与自己从小相伴情同姐妹的春香。她再也控制不住自己的情绪，流着眼泪，脱口喊了一声：“娘啊！”

Du Liniang glanced at the old lady by the moonlight and was taken aback. She wondered, “How strange! This lady looks just like my mother.” Turning around, she asked, “May I ask Your Ladyship where you came from?” With a sigh, the old lady said, “From Yangzhou we came and my lord is the envoy of Huai’an. As the war broke out, we fled before the nomads’ advancing troops.”

With a mixed feeling of joy and grief, Du Liniang turned around and tears streamed down her face. She thought, “She is my mother. But shall I make known myself?” Turning around, she found the young girl was right there by her side. By the moonlight, she found out that this young girl was none other than her maid Chunxiang. Unable to hold back her feelings, she cried in tears, “Mother!”

甄氏吓了一跳，语无伦次地说道："你是我女儿？你现形了？娘怠慢你了，春香，快撒纸钱！"春香也吓得双手发抖，连忙撒纸钱。

丽娘拉住老夫人的手，哭着说道："娘，女儿不是鬼。"甄氏避开丽娘，说道："你不是鬼？那我叫你三声，你答应三声，一声要比一声高。"说罢唤了三声。丽娘心中伤悲，只好含泪答应，一声比一声低，一声比一声哽咽。甄氏的手不由地又抖了起来，哭道："你是鬼。"丽娘还想凑上前去，甄氏和春香却避得远远的。

Terribly frightened, Lady Du said incoherently, "Can you be my daughter? You make this apparition because I neglected your offerings. Chunxiang, throw some paper coins out on the ground!" Chunxiang was also frightened. With trembling hands, Chunxiang started throwing out paper coins at once.

Grasping the old lady by the hand, Du Liniang wept and said, "Mother, I'm no ghost." Lady Du dodged and said, "You're telling me you aren't a ghost? Well, I'll call your name three times. If you're not a ghost, answer me louder each time." With this, Lady Du called out Du Liniang's name three times. Overwhelmed with sadness, Du Liniang answered with tears in her eyes, but as she was choking with sobs, her voice faded away, becoming lower and lower each time she answered. Lady Du's hands started trembling uncontrollably as she cried, "You are a ghost!" Du Liniang stepped forward, but Lady Du and Chunxiang dodged in fear.

石道姑端着油灯走了过来，院子里顿时显得明亮起来。她看见甄氏和春香，吃了一惊，问道：“呀，老夫人和春香从哪里来？”

丽娘连忙说道：“老姑姑快来，我娘正怕我呢。”石道姑知道她们害怕，便举起油灯，照着丽娘的脸，对甄氏说道：“老夫人仔细看看，小姐不是和当年一个样么？”甄氏走过来细细地端详了一番，忽然一把抱住丽娘，含泪说道：“女儿，你就是鬼，娘也舍不得你了！”母女相认，不觉痛哭起来。

Mother Stone entered, holding a lamp, and the yard was immediately lit up. Greatly surprised as she saw Lady Du and Chunxiang, she asked, “Why? How did my lady and Chunxiang find our house?”

“Mother Stone,” said Du Liniang, “please help me. My mother has got a shock.” Knowing that Lady Du and Chunxiang must have been frightened by what they had seen, Mother Stone held up the lamp to Du Liniang and said to Lady Du, “Look closer by the lamp. Is it not the face you knew?” Moving closer to Du Liniang, Lady Du examined her face for a while. Suddenly she embraced Du Liniang and wept, saying, “My child, I wouldn’t leave you again even if you were a ghost.” With this, both the mother and the daughter started crying bitterly.

石道姑便将事情的来龙去脉一一告诉了甄氏和春香，二人听后面面相觑，甄氏还不肯相信，回头问春香道："难道真有这样的事？" 春香见小姐言语平静温柔，和生前没什么两样，心中早就相信了，点头答道："是小姐，不然还会有这么漂亮的鬼吗？" 甄氏又抱住丽娘大哭道："我的儿呀！" 母女二人又痛哭了一场。

随后，甄氏和春香便在临安住了下来，与丽娘一起，等待柳梦梅的消息。

Mother Stone told Lady Du and Chunxiang the whole story of Du Liniang and Liu Mengmei. Hearing the story, Lady Du and Chunxiang eyed each other with the deepest suspicion. Still finding it hard to believe it, Lady Du turned around and asked Chunxiang, "Can her story be true?" Chunxiang had already believed it, as she found that the way Du Liniang spoke and acted was no different with that when she was alive. "I think so," said Chunxiang, "for how there be a ghost as pretty as she!" Pulling Du Liniang into her arms, Lady Du wept again, "My dear child!"

Then, Lady Du and Chunxiang put themselves up in Lin'an with Du Liniang and waited for the news of Liu Mengmei.

柳梦梅风尘仆仆地赶到扬州，见不到杜宝，只好启程前往淮安。他来到淮安城外，只见城门大开，处处张灯结彩，根本不像战乱的样子。

原来，陈最良来到李全军中，按照杜宝的吩咐，把信交给了李全的夫人杨氏。信中说皇上已经敕封杨氏为讨金娘娘，并答应只要李全归降，就保他夫妻荣华富贵，杨氏看后大乐，答应投降南宋。李全是个最怕老婆的人，不敢反对，况且自己在大金国也受排挤，便顺水推舟降了南宋，淮扬一带转危为安。

杜宝平敌有功，被朝廷提升为宰相，陈最良被任命为黄门奏事官。

After having traveled far and experienced lots of hardships, Liu Mengmei arrived in Yangzhou only to find that Du Bao had transferred to Huai'an. Having no other choice, he had to move on forward to Huai'an. As he reached Huai'an, he found the gate of Huai'an city was wide open and lanterns and colorful banners could be found everywhere. There was nothing there that looked like wartime at all.

Here is how it went. When Chen Zuiliang got to Li Quan's camp, as he was told, he handed Du Bao's letter to Li Quan's wife Lady Yang. In the letter, Du Bao said that His Majesty had granted her ladyship the title of Gold Licking Lady and assured them of high position and wealth if Li Quan surrendered. Lady Yang was overjoyed at this and agreed to surrender. Li Quan was a henpecked man and dared not to go against her. As Li Quan was somewhat excluded in the Jin Court, he just made use of this opportunity and surrendered to the Southern Song. As a consequence of this, Huaiyang went out of danger and became safe.

Du Bao was promoted to be the Grand Chancellor for his meritorious service in quelling the enemy and Chen Zuiliang was appointed as the Yellow Gate Herald.

柳梦梅得知此事，心中大喜，连忙来到府衙门口，只见将士们正在大摆宴席，庆贺太平。

柳梦梅本想直接走进去见杜宝，又担心冒昧，怕杜宝不会认自己这个从未谋面的女婿。他整了整衣冠，对着门口的将士行礼道："杜老爷女婿求见。"守门的将士一愣，问道："当真？""秀才不说假话。"柳梦梅答道。那将士看了他几眼，便转身走进去禀告。

片刻之后，将士出来对柳梦梅说道："老爷军务繁忙，叫你自便。"柳梦梅问道："老爷难道是拜客去了么？"那将士答道："今日老爷要和文武官僚吃太平宴呢。"

Liu Mengmei was overjoyed at the news. As he came to the entrance of the yamen, he found out all the soldiers were setting the tables to celebrate the arrival of peace.

Liu Mengmei originally wanted to go and see Du Bao, but he was worried that it might be indiscreet, fearing that Du Bao probably would not accept him as his son-in-law. Straightening up his hat and clothes and bowing to the attendants guarding the gate, he said, "The son-in-law of Lord Du requests an interview with Lord Du." Shocked, the attendants asked, "Are you kidding?" "A scholar tells no lies," answered Liu Mengmei. One attendant looked at him a couple of times and, turning around, entered to report the matter.

Before long, the attendant came out and said to Liu Mengmei, "Lord Du is occupied with military affairs. Go somewhere and please yourself." "Is Lord Du receiving guests?" asked Liu Mengmei. "Today, all officials and officers are to attend the peace celebration banquet," answered the attendant.

柳梦梅站在那里，傻傻地想道："原来如此，只怕一会儿见岳父大人，还要考一首《太平宴诗》呢，我暂且在这门房里打好腹稿，免得到时候出丑。"他想了很久，腹稿已经打好了，杜宝还没有派人来叫他，衙门里飘来一阵阵酒菜的香味，饿得他肚子咕咕直叫。

柳梦梅只好央求将士再进去禀告一声，那将士不肯，柳梦梅便和他争吵了起来，吵闹声惊动了酒席上的杜宝，他恼羞成怒，走了出来，说道："我哪里有什么女婿？混账！"说罢吩咐中军拿下柳梦梅。

Still standing there, muddleheaded, Liu Mengmei thought to himself, "I see. Probably when I meet my father-in-law, I'll be asked to improvise a poem on the topic as 'The Banquet of Peace'. What if I fail to compose one on the spot? Better prepare for it while I wait in the doorman's room." After thinking for a while, a poem had been written in his head. But Du Bao had not sent for him yet. His stomach was making noise as the scent of food and wine came up to his nostrils.

Liu Mengmei had to ask the attendant to go and inform Lord Du of his coming, but the attendant refused his request. At this, Liu Mengmei and the attendant started to quarrel, which alerted Du Bao who was still at the banquet table. Du Bao came out, outraged, and shouted, "Confound it! Whence comes this son-in-law of mine?" So saying, he ordered the adjutant to have Liu Mengmei tied up.

庆功宴结束，杜宝便离开淮安，回到家中。他吩咐将柳梦梅带上堂来，骂道："你是什么人？犯了法，还在相府阶前站着不

跪？”柳梦梅答道：“岭南柳梦梅，是老大人的女婿。”

杜宝一听便火冒三丈，冷笑道：“你这个打秋风的恶棍！我女儿已经亡故三年了，生前并未许亲，哪有什么女婿？可笑，可恨！”说罢不等柳梦梅争辩，便吩咐手下人搜他的包袱，只见包裹中别无他物，只有一条破布单，一幅画像。

杜宝见到画像，大吃一惊，说道：“这不是我女儿的春容吗？你从何得来？”

When the banquet was over, Du Bao left Huai'an and returned home. Then he ordered that Liu Mengmei be brought to his Grand Chancellor's residence. At the sight of Liu Mengmei, Du Bao cursed, "You miserable beggar, who are you? Now that you have offended the law, why don't you kneel?" "My name is Liu Mengmei," replied Liu Mengmei. "I'm a scholar from the South of the Five Ridges. I'm Your Excellency's son-in-law."

Du Bao became mad at once. Laughing grimly, he said, "You scoundrel! My daughter died three years ago. And never had I accepted any betrothal gifts from any family, nor had she been engaged to anyone when she was alive. How could I have acquired a son-in-law? Your claim is ridiculous and abhorrent!" Before Liu Mengmei had the chance to argue, Du Bao told his adjutants to search his bundle. As they untied Liu Mengmei's bundle, they found nothing but a torn bed-sheet and a portrait of a girl.

Du Bao was surprised at the sight of the portrait. He said, "It is my daughter's portrait. How did you get it?"

杜宝捻着胡须，沉吟了片刻，便问柳梦梅："你可曾到过南安，见过石道姑吗？"柳梦梅见他问起石道姑，以为杜宝见到春容，相信了他的话，便连忙答应说认识。杜宝又问道："可认得陈教授么？""认得。"杜宝冷笑一声道："天网恢恢，疏而不漏，原来你就是那个盗坟贼。快给我拿下，打！"

柳梦梅叫道："谁敢打我？"杜宝气得七窍生烟，喝道："你这贼汉，还不从实招来！"柳梦梅反驳道："'拿贼见赃'，你有什么证据说我是贼？"

Du Bao twirled his moustache and thought for a moment. Then he asked, "Have you ever been to Nan'an and come to know a Mother Stone?" When asked about whether he knew Mother Stone, Liu Mengmei thought that Du Bao had believed his words at the sight of the portrait. Quickly he said he did. "Do you happen to know a Mr. Chen as well?" came Du Bao's next inquiry. "Yes, I do," answered Liu Mengmei. With a sneer, Du Bao said, "No one can escape from its boundlessness. So you're the grave-robber. Drag him out and give him a good lashing."

"Dare you beat me?" shouted Liu Mengmei. Foaming with rage, Du Bao shouted, "You thief, make a confession of your crime!" Liu Mengmei retorted, "When Your Excellency names someone a thief, you'd better get hold of the stolen goods. What proof do you have to conclude that I'm a thief?"

柳梦梅据理力争道：“你的证据不就是这幅画像吗？如果不是我开棺救你女儿出来，她还不会还魂复活呢！”

杜宝根本不理会他说的那一套，见他承认开棺一事，便认定他是盗坟贼。他叫手下在纸上写下供词："犯人一名柳梦梅，开棺劫坟者斩。"并叫柳梦梅在下面画押，柳梦梅不肯画押，大声嚷道："生员并不犯奸盗，何况，令爱她还活着！"杜宝喝道："胡说！陈最良说我女儿尸骨都被你抛到水池中去了！"

柳梦梅听了这话，仰天长叹道："我对小姐一片真情，陈最良哪里知道！"

Liu Mengmei continued to argue strongly on just grounds, "You think the portrait is a solid proof? Had I not opened your daughter's coffin and taken her out of the grave, she would not have come back to life!"

Du Bao was paying no attention to what Liu Mengmei was talking about and, seeing that Liu Mengmei had acknowledged the fact of opening the coffin, firmly believed that he was the very grave-robber. He had his secretary write down what Liu Mengmei said on a sheet of paper, and with his verdict: "Convict Liu Mengmei, having opened the coffin and robbed the grave, is to be executed." With this, he handed it to Liu Mengmei and ordered him to sign his name. Liu Mengmei refused to sign his name. Putting up a struggle, Liu Mengmei shouted, "I committed neither adultery nor theft. Moreover, your daughter is still alive!" "Nonsense!" Du Bao thundered. "Master Chen told me you've thrown my daughter's bones into the pool!"

Upon hearing this, Liu Mengmei lifted up his eyes and sighed, "The pains I suffered for Miss Du is only known to heaven and earth. What does Chen Zuiliang know about it?"

任凭柳梦梅如何辩解、叫嚷，杜宝都无动于衷，他命令手下人将柳梦梅高高吊起，用荆条狠狠地抽打，柳梦梅痛苦不堪，发出一声声惨叫，好端端的一个相国府，顿时弄得鬼哭狼嚎。

杜宝见柳梦梅被拷打一番之后，还是不肯画押，正在生气，忽然看见一个人闯了进来，原来是主考官苗舜宾，后面跟着堂候官，手里捧着冠带、状元袍。杜宝还没明白过来是怎么回事，便听柳梦梅叫唤道："苗大人，快救门生一命！"

Du Bao just turned a deaf ear no matter how loudly Liu Mengmei shouted to justify himself. He ordered his men to hang him up and beat him hard with peach twigs. In pain, Liu Mengmei gave out sad, shrill cries. Immediately the Grand Chancellor's office was filled with dreary cries and screams.

Though he was tortured, Liu Mengmei still refused to sign his name. While Du Bao was in a cross temper, he suddenly saw some one break in. It was Miao Shunbin the Chief Examiner, followed by a lieutenant holding a hat and a robe. Before Du Bao could figured out what was going on, Liu Mengmei shouted, "Oh, Master Miao, Help your student! Help!"

苗舜宾施礼道：“老公相且住手，有登科录在此，这被吊的柳梦梅，是御笔亲题的新科状元。”杜宝不肯相信，苗舜宾又说道：“晚生亲自取中的，老公相怎么打起状元郎来了。”便吩咐军士将柳梦梅放了下来。

苗舜宾准备询问事情原委，只听柳梦梅答道：“他是我丈人。”杜宝在一旁冷笑道：“只怕状元不是他，若果真是他，怎么没等发榜，就跑到淮扬来招摇撞骗？”柳梦梅答道：“令爱叫我来淮扬打探您的消息，您反而将好心当成驴肝肺——现在我可是您的女婿了？”杜宝气冲冲地说道：“谁认你做女婿了！”

“Please stay your hand, Your Excellency,” said Miao Shunbin. “Here is the Scholars’ Register. The man hanging there, Liu Mengmei, is the first choice of the royal pen.” Seeing that Du Bao was not going to believe it, Miao Shunbin continued, “It was my humble self who recommended him. How should Your Excellency beat *zhuangyuan*?” With this, Miao Shunbin told his men to lift down Liu Mengmei.

As Miao Shunbin was about to inquire about the details, Liu Mengmei said, “He is my father-in-law.” Du Bao said with a grin, “I just can’t believe he is the *zhuangyuan*. If he were, how could he have roamed into Huaiyang instead of waiting in the capital for the announcement?” Liu Mengmei said, “Your daughter bade me to go to Huaiyang to inquire about the news about you. But our good intentions met with ill treatment. Now will you accept me as your son-in-law?” “No, never,” answered Du Bao furiously.

苗舜宾笑道：“老公相怎么跟自己的女婿生起气来了？”杜宝“哼”了一声，道：“只怪我没有早点将这个盗坟贼上报朝廷。”不管苗舜宾如何劝说，他总是一口咬定柳梦梅是盗坟贼。

柳梦梅讥笑他道：“你身为宰相，却是非不分，把个好女婿当做了贼。总有一天你会对我客气起来的！”说罢朝杜宝拱了拱手，道：“您女婿赴状元宴去了！”他整理好冠袍，大步流星地走了。

“Your Excellency, there is no reason to get so irritated with your son-in-law,” said Miao Shunbin with a smile. With a snort, Du Bao said, “I only regret that I didn’t keep this grave-robber behind bars till his execution was ratified.” No matter how Miao Shunbin persuaded him, Du Bao just insisted that Liu Mengmei was a grave-robber.

Liu Mengmei said with a sneer, “Though you’re the Grand Chancellor, you confuse truth with falsehood and take me as a robber. The day is sure to come when you’ll be nice to me!” Then he made an obeisance to Du Bao by cupping one hand in the other before his chest and added, “Sir, your son-in-law is going to attend the imperial banquet.” Straightening up his hat and robe, he walked out with vigorous strides.

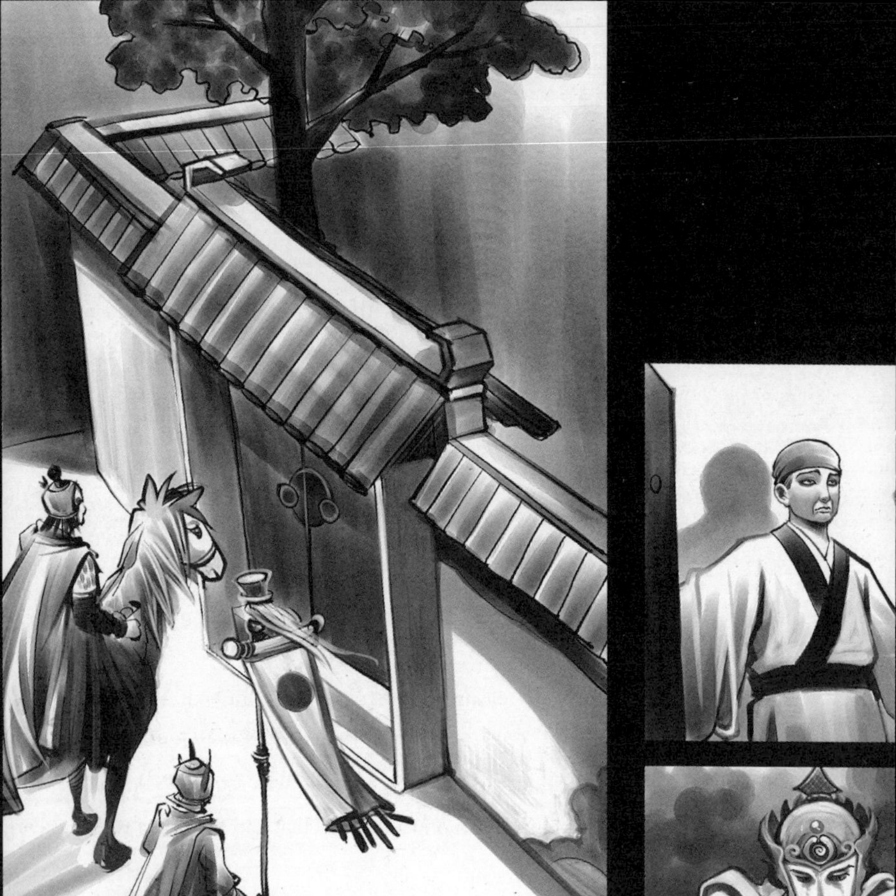

丽娘和甄氏自从母女重逢之后，朝夕相伴，生活也颇为惬意，只是父亲和柳郎尚无音信，她心中很担忧。

这天丽娘正和春香在闺房中做活儿，只见甄氏急急忙忙走了进来，说道："女儿，我听到门外有人大声喧嚷，好像说新科状元正是岭南柳梦梅呢！"丽娘听了，喜形于色，问道："真的吗？"话未说完，石道姑也走了进来："夫人，小姐，外面有人敲门呢，好像是官军的声音，快出去看看吧。"

说罢，石道姑走出去打开了院门，只见门外站着两个军校，手持黄旗，说道："这可是状元府第？我们是来传圣旨的。"

Since Du Liniang and her mother Lady Du got reunited, they kept each other's company day and night and led a pretty comfortable life. The only one thing that concerned Du Liniang was that there was still no word from her father and Liu Mengmei.

One day, while Du Liniang and Chunxiang were doing some needlework in the boudoir, Lady Du rushed in and said, "I heard a hubbub going on outside in the streets, as if saying the new *zhuangyuan* is Liu Mengmei from the South of the Five Ridges!" Beaming up with pleasure, Du Liniang asked, "Can that be true?" Before Du Liniang finished her words, Mother Stone entered in a great rush. "Madame, Miss," said Mother Stone, "there are some people there knocking at our gate. They look like sergeants from the imperial court. Better come on quick and have a look."

So saying, Mother Stone went out of the room and opened the gate. Two sergeants were standing at the gate bearing bright yellow flags. "Is this the new *zhuangyuan*'s home?" said the sergeants. "We're here to send the imperial edict."

丽娘听说有人来传圣旨，连忙穿好衣服，走出来问道：“请问官爷，新科状元可是岭南柳梦梅？”军校答道：“正是柳梦梅，他中了状元，被杜相爷当成盗墓贼，吊在宰相府打呢。”“哪个杜相爷？”“就是退了敌兵的淮扬杜安抚，如今升为宰相了。”

丽娘还未答话，甄氏便在后面说道：“谢天谢地，老爷平安回京了。他哪里知道女儿重生之事？”丽娘问道：“状元郎现在在哪里？”军校答道：“正在万岁爷面前闹不清呢。”

Upon hearing that some people had come with the imperial edict, Du Liniang quickly got herself properly dressed and came out. “May I presume to ask if the new *zhuangyuan* is Liu Mengmei from the South of the Five Ridges?” asked Du Liniang. “Yes,” replied the sergeants, “Liu Mengmei is the new *zhuangyuan*, but Grand Chancellor Du thought he is a grave-robber and is now having him hung up and whipped with peach-tree twigs.” “Which Grand Chancellor Du?” asked Du Liniang. The sergeants said, “Envoy Du of Huaiyang who has subdued the Jin troops. Now he has been promoted to the Grand Chancellor.”

“Thank heavens,” Lady Du said before Du Liniang spoke. “Father has returned to the capital in safety. And of course, he couldn’t have believed in such a thing as her daughter’s resurrection.” Du Liniang asked, “But how about Mr. Liu?” The sergeants answered, “The lieutenants have snatched him off to meet His Majesty.”

原来，杜宝在柳梦梅走后，便上了一本奏折给皇上，说杜丽娘复活是妖怪作孽，柳梦梅是盗墓贼，不可以做状元。柳梦梅得知此事，也向皇帝上了一本奏折，将前因后果一一说明。二人各持己见，互不相让。皇上都看呆了，也不相信此事是真的。后来还是黄门奏事官陈最良建议，要杜宝、柳梦梅与杜丽娘三人在金殿上当面核对，辨明是非。

军校向杜丽娘说明上述情况后，道："杜小姐，皇上命你明日五更三点到金殿当面对质，你要早做准备。"杜丽娘心中欢喜，对甄氏说道："娘，爹爹高升，柳郎高中，真是双喜临门啊!"

It turned out that, after Liu Mengmei was taken away, Du Bao had sent in a report to His Majesty, saying that Du Liniang's resurrection was nothing but the evildoing of a wicked spirit, and Liu Mengmei was a grave-robber and was not qualified for the title of *zhuangyuan*. Liu Mengmei had also submitted a report to His Majesty to defend himself. Each stuck to his own view. Even His Majesty was confused and could hardly believe it. It happened that Chen Zuiliang, the Yellow Gate Herald, suggested that Du Bao, Liu Mengmei and Du Liniang come to face each other in the Court so that His Majesty could determine a verdict.

Having made it clear to Du Liniang, the sergeants said, "Miss Du, His Majesty commands you to be present at the Court at the third notch of the fifth drum to meet your father and Liu Mengmei. You'd better make preparations in advance." Very much pleased, Du Liniang said to Lady Du, "Mother, Father has been promoted, and Mr. Liu has succeeded. A double blessing has ascended upon our family!"

金殿对质的这一刻来到了，杜宝和柳梦梅都早早地来到皇宫，两人在宫门不期而遇，柳梦梅便行礼道：“拜见岳父大人！”杜宝把脸扭向一边，说道：“谁是你岳丈！”杜宝爱理不理，独自向金殿走去。

这时候，丽娘也来到了皇宫，她走在御道上，心情非常紧张，她不知道自己还魂复活之事，能不能得到皇帝的相信，也不知道自己和柳郎的婚姻，能不能得到皇帝和父亲的许可。

When there came the face-to-face time at the Court, Du Bao and Liu Mengmei arrived at the imperial palace in good time. As they met by chance at the entrance of the imperial palace, Liu Mengmei offered a salute, saying, “My respects to Father-in-law!” Du Bao looked away and said, “Who is your father-in-law!” Looking cold and indifferent, Du Bao walked off to the Court alone.

Soon Du Liniang arrived at the imperial palace too. While she walked down the royal street, she became extremely nervous, having not the least idea whether His Majesty would believe in her resurrection and whether His Majesty and her father would grant permission to her marriage with Liu Mengmei.

陈最良将丽娘领入金殿，丽娘连忙跪下呼道："皇上万岁，万万岁。"高高的御阶上传来了皇帝的声音："平身。"丽娘紧张地站起身来。

皇上命杜宝、柳梦梅辨识杜丽娘。柳梦梅马上站了出来，大呼道："俺的丽娘妻啊！"杜宝却冷冷地站在一边，打量了丽娘一番，大声说道："这鬼真的一模一样，大胆！大胆！"说罢便回身跪下，奏道："皇上，臣的女儿已亡三年，这是花妖狐媚作怪，千万不要放过她！"只见柳梦梅在一旁冷笑道："好狠心的父亲！"

Chen Zuiliang led Du Liniang into the Court. Du Liniang knelt down to the throne and said, "Long live our emperor!" "Rise to your feet," came His Majesty's voice from the throne. Then Du Liniang rose to her feet nervously.

Then the emperor told Du Bao and Liu Mengmei to step out and identify Du Liniang. Stepping out, Liu Mengmei shouted, "She is my dear wife, Du Liniang!" Standing aside indifferently, Du Bao sized Du Liniang up and said in a loud voice, "What a devil! What insolence! What insolence!" With this, he turned around to face the throne and knelt to make a report, "Your Majesty, my only daughter died three years ago. Though this one is cast in her mold, it can only be an impersonation of a flower spirit or a fox spirit. Du Bao begs not to let her off lightly!" With a sneer, Liu Mengmei said, "What a father of a stone heart!"

皇上见杜宝和柳梦梅仍争执不休，便传下圣旨："朕听说人行有影，鬼形怕镜，黄门官，定时台上有一面秦朝照胆镜，你立刻领着杜丽娘前去照镜，看花荫之下，有无踪影，立刻回奏。"陈最良答应一声，便领着杜丽娘下了金殿。

片刻之后，只见陈最良回奏道："杜丽娘有影有踪，确系人身。"皇上沉吟了片刻，便降旨道："杜丽娘既是人身，立刻将前亡后化的事情奏陈上来。"杜丽娘便一五一十地将自己因梦成痴，因情而亡，最后起死回生，与柳梦梅私自结为夫妻之事叙述了一遍。

Seeing Du Bao and Liu Mengmei get into a terrific argument, His Majesty said, "I, your sovereign, hear that man walks with his shadow, and ghosts are afraid of looking into the mirrors. On the sundial platform we have a mirror with penetrating power handed down from the Qin Dynasty. The Yellow Gate Herald will lead Du Liniang to the mirror and then let her walk through the flower beds to see if she leaves any trace. Make a report afterward." Chen Zuiliang responded at once and showed Du Liniang out of the Court.

Before long, Chen Zuiliang returned and reported, "Du Liniang has a perfect shadow and walks with a trace behind. No doubt she is a human being." After a moment of meditation, His Majesty said, "Since it has been proved that Du Liniang is a human being, she can make a report of her experience of death and rebirth." Then Du Liniang gave a full account of how she had become obsessed because of a dream, how she had died of yearning for love, how she had been brought back to life, and how she had got married with Liu Mengmei secretly.

杜宝依然不肯认丽娘。丽娘非常伤心，含泪说道：“爹啊，你不认女儿，有娘在呢。”

正在这时候，甄氏闯入宫来，跪奏皇上。杜宝一见甄氏，吓了一跳，他连忙跪下向皇上奏道：“万岁爷，臣妻早就死于扬州贼寇之手，这肯定是妖鬼捏造的，故意欺瞒皇上。”甄氏不等杜宝再说下去，便将自己逃生至临安，与女儿深夜相遇，母女重逢一事细细向皇上奏明。

皇上听完甄氏的陈述，便下旨道："朕听甄氏母女所奏，杜丽娘重生无疑，黄门官，将他们一家四口送到午门外，父子夫妻相认，回家成亲。"众人都大呼皇帝英明，叩头谢恩，只有杜宝一言不发。

Du Bao still refused to accept Du Liniang as his daughter. Heart-broken, Du Liniang said, "Father, though you wouldn't accept me, Mother has."

Right at this moment, Lady Du entered the palace, knelt before the throne and was about to make a report. Du Bao was terribly startled by the appearance of Lady Du. Throwing himself on his knees before the emperor, Du Bao reported, "Your Majesty's humble servant Du Bao begs to declare that his wife had already died at the hands of the bandits in Yangzhou. This one here must be another product of the devil in an attempt to fool Your Majesty." Before Du Bao could finish, Lady Du made a clear report to His Majesty on how she had fled to Lin'an and how she had met and got reunited with her daughter one night.

Having heard Lady Du's account of her experience, His Majesty said, "I, your sovereign, have listened carefully to Du Liniang's report and my doubts about her resurrection are now cleared. The Yellow Gate Herald shall escort them out of the palace gate and see to it that father and child, husband and wife, become reconciled, and a formal wedding shall be arranged for the young couple." All present shouted "Long live our emperor!" and kowtowed to express their gratitude. But Du Bao alone remained silent.

出了金殿，丽娘唤道："爹爹，认了女儿吧。"杜宝气冲冲地说道："离了柳梦梅，我就回去认你。"丽娘便拉了拉柳梦梅的衣襟，示意他向杜宝下拜，柳梦梅也在气头上，不肯下拜。丽娘无奈，只好拉着柳梦梅的手，按着他的肩膀拜了下去。

甄氏和陈最良也劝说了杜宝一番。杜宝见柳梦梅下跪在地，口呼"老丈人"，便勉强答应了一声，终于相认了。这时候，皇帝又派官员来降旨封赠，夫妻团圆，父女相认。一场生死相恋的爱情终于收获了圆满的结局。

When they were out of the imperial palace, Du Liniang said, "Father, won't you recognize your daughter?" "Get rid of that Liu Mengmei and I'll take you home as my daughter," Du Bao replied angrily. Hearing this, Du Liniang pulled Liu Mengmei by the garments and motioned him to make a bow to Father-in-law. At this moment Liu Mengmei was in a fit of anger too, and refused to do so. Having no choice, Du Liniang had to pull Liu Mengmei by the hand and pressed him on the shoulder to make him bend his back and clasp his hands.

Lady Du and Chen Zuiliang also tried their best to persuade Du Bao to accept Liu Mengmei as his son-in-law. As he saw Liu Mengmei calling him "Father-in-law" on his knees, Du Bao finally responded with a "yes" and accepted him, though it was with some difficulty. At this point there came the imperial decree that the family be reunited and each one of the family be conferred with a title. Husband and wife got reunited and father and daughter recognized each other. And a life-and-death love came to a happy ending.

郑重声明